NINETEENTH AND TWENTIETH CENTURY VERSE

An anthology of sixteen poets
Edited by Chris Woodhead

Oxford University Press

Oxford University Press, Walton Street, Oxford OX2 6DP

Oxford New York Toronto
Delhi Bombay Calcutta Madras Karachi
Petaling Jaya Singapore Hong Kong Tokyo
Nairobi Dar es Salaam Cape Town
Melbourne Auckland

and associated companies in
Berlin Ibadan

Oxford is a trade mark of Oxford University Press

First published 1984
Reprinted 1986, 1987, 1989

ISBN 0 19 831247 4

Set by Rowland Phototypesetting Ltd
Bury St Edmunds, Suffolk
Printed in Great Britain by
The Bath Press, Avon

CONTENTS

PREFACE

My aim in compiling this anthology has been to introduce readers to the most significant poets of the last two hundred years. I would have liked to include selections from the works of Coleridge, Byron, Shelley, Emily Brontë and Matthew Arnold, but limitations of space made this impossible. It could certainly be argued that each of these poets deserves to be included: they have been omitted because their best poems tend either to be very long or in various ways inaccessible to modern readers. Such decisions are inevitably personal, and I can only apologize to any reader who finds that his or her favourite poet is missing from the following pages.

I have tried with each poet to select poems which are both rich and important in themselves and representative of the poet's central, most characteristic concerns. The introductory comments on each poet fall into two sections: firstly, a brief biographical outline of important events in the poet's life; and, secondly, some general remarks about the main themes and style of the poet's work. Notes on each poem are printed at the end of the book. These notes supply information about the meanings of words and references which might be obscure, but, and this is perhaps more important, they also contain questions which are intended to develop personal understanding and appreciation of the poems. My assumption here is that it is sometimes helpful to be led into a poem, but these questions can, of course, be ignored by anyone who finds them intrusive.

There are two dangers to be avoided in reading poetry: that of rejecting a poem out of hand because it does not make any sense to you on a first reading, and that of believing poems are there to be 'solved' as a crossword puzzle can be solved. 'The secret of being a poet', Seamus Heaney tells us, 'lies in summoning the energies of words.' The secret of reading poems lies in responding to the 'energies' which the poet has summoned, in feeling your way patiently into the words, images and the rhythms he has chosen to use. The poems you are about to read demand such patience, but you will find, I hope, that they reward it, too.

WILLIAM BLAKE
1757–1827

William Blake was a Londoner. At the age of fifteen, he was apprenticed to an engraver and six years later he became a student at the Royal Academy of Art. Throughout his life he painted, and he illustrated many of his poems with etchings and engravings. His wife, Catherine, was illiterate when they married, but after Blake had taught her to read and write, she helped with his etching and bookbinding and developed a talent for drawing. He published several collections of poems, including the *Songs of Innocence* and the *Songs of Experience*, both illustrated by his etchings and coloured individually by hand.

Blake spent all but three years of his life in London. Neither his writing nor engraving and painting were widely appreciated and he was always hard up. He was acutely conscious of political and religious oppression and of how the lives of the poor were ruined by fear and disease. He supported the French Revolution and the English Radical reformers and was once tried and acquitted on a charge of treason after he had been supposedly heard to curse the King and praise Napoleon. Later he became disillusioned by Napoleon's tyranny.

Blake was a profoundly religious man and his spiritual life inspired much of his writing and painting. Though a Christian, he did not accept the orthodox doctrines and authority of the Church of England and, as time went on, developed his own symbolic version of the faith.

The *Songs of Innocence*, as the title suggests, present a world in which a child delights in life, protected from all danger by a parent figure (a mother or father, sometimes God or an angel). In the *Songs of Experience* fear has replaced security. Relationships between parents and children or between lovers tend to be unhappy, spoilt by a lack of trust and understanding. All hope of protective love has disappeared, and authority figures condemn the sexual expression of love which had been seen in some of the *Songs of Innocence* as the natural expression of the 'joy' of innocence. The two collections are a record of Blake's thinking and feeling as he was forced to give up the happy, joyful view of life presented in the *Songs of Innocence* for the more painful vision of the *Songs of Experience*. They exist together as a statement of what life might or should be, and what in fact it is, like. When Blake published *The Songs of Innocence and Experience* in one volume, the title was followed by the words 'Showing the two contrary states of the human soul'.

Blake has, as the later poet T. S. Eliot says, 'a peculiar honesty, which, in a world too frightened to be honest, is peculiarly terrifying. It is an honesty against which the world conspires because it is unpleasant. Blake's poetry has the unpleasantness of great poetry.'

SONGS OF INNOCENCE

The Lamb

    Little lamb, who made thee?
    Dost thou know who made thee
Gave thee life and bid thee feed
By the stream and o'er the mead—
Gave thee clothing of delight,   5
Softest clothing, woolly, bright,
Gave thee such a tender voice,
Making all the vales rejoice?
    Little lamb, who made thee,
    Dost thou know who made thee? 10

    Little lamb, I'll tell thee,
    Little lamb, I'll tell thee!
He is callèd by thy name,
For he calls himself a Lamb;
He is meek and he is mild,   15
He became a little child:
I a child, and thou a lamb,
We are callèd by his name.
    Little lamb, God bless thee,
    Little lamb, God bless thee! 20

The Chimney Sweeper

When my mother died I was very young,
And my father sold me while yet my tongue
Could scarcely cry ''weep! 'weep! 'weep! 'weep!'
So your chimneys I sweep, and in soot I sleep.

There's little Tom Dacre, who cried when his head,   5
That curled like a lamb's back, was shaved; so I said,
'Hush, Tom! never mind it, for when your head's bare
You know that the soot cannot spoil your white hair.'

And so he was quiet, and that very night,
As Tom was a-sleeping, he had such a sight!—   10
That thousands of sweepers, Dick, Joe, Ned and Jack,
Were all of them locked up in coffins of black;

And by came an angel who had a bright key,
And he opened the coffins and set them all free;
Then down a green plain, leaping, laughing, they run,   15
And wash in a river, and shine in the sun.

Then naked and white, all their bags left behind,
They rise upon clouds and sport in the wind.
And the angel told Tom, if he'd be a good boy,
He'd have God for his father, and never want joy.   20

And so Tom awoke, and we rose in the dark,
And got with our bags and our brushes to work.
Though the morning was cold, Tom was happy and warm;
So if all do their duty, they need not fear harm.

The Little Boy Lost

'Father, Father, where are you going?
O do not walk so fast!
Speak, Father, speak to your little boy,
Or else I shall be lost.'

The night was dark, no father was there,   5
The child was wet with dew;
The mire was deep, and the child did weep,
And away the vapour flew.

The Little Boy Found

The little boy lost in the lonely fen,
Led by the wandering light,
Began to cry, but God, ever nigh,
Appeared like his father in white.

He kissed the child and by the hand led,   5
And to his mother brought,
Who in sorrow pale through the lonely dale
Her little boy weeping sought.

Nurse's Song

When the voices of children are heard on the green,
And laughing is heard on the hill,
My heart is at rest within my breast,
And everything else is still.

'Then come home, my children, the sun is gone down,   5
And the dews of night arise;
Come, come, leave off play, and let us away
Till the morning appears in the skies.'

'No, no, let us play, for it is yet day,
And we cannot go to sleep;   10
Besides, in the sky the little birds fly,
And the hills are all covered with sheep.'

'Well, well, go and play till the light fades away,
And then go home to bed.'
The little ones leaped and shouted and laughed   15
And all the hills echoèd.

A Dream

Once a dream did weave a shade,
O'er my angel-guarded bed,
That an emmet lost its way
Where on grass methought I lay.

Troubled, wildered and forlorn,   5
Dark, benighted, travel-worn,
Over many a tangled spray,
All heart-broke I heard her say:

'O, my children! do they cry?
Do they hear their father sigh?   10
Now they look abroad to see,
Now return and weep for me.'

Pitying, I dropped a tear;
But I saw a glow-worm near,
Who replied, 'What wailing wight   15
Calls the watchman of the night?

'I am set to light the ground,
While the beetle goes his round.
Follow now the beetle's hum;
Little wanderer, hie thee home.'   20

On Another's Sorrow

Can I see another's woe,
And not be in sorrow too?
Can I see another's grief,
And not seek for kind relief?

Can I see a falling tear,   5
And not feel my sorrow's share?
Can a father see his child
Weep, nor be with sorrow filled?

Can a mother sit and hear
An infant groan, an infant fear?   10
No, no! never can it be!
Never, never can it be!

And can he who smiles on all
Hear the wren with sorrows small,
Hear the small bird's grief and care,   15
Hear the woes that infants bear,

And not sit beside the nest
Pouring pity in their breast,
And not sit the cradle near
Weeping tear on infant's tear,   20

And not sit both night and day,
Wiping all our tears away?
O, no, never can it be,
Never, never can it be!

He doth give his joy to all,   25
He becomes an infant small.
He becomes a man of woe,
He doth feel the sorrow too.

Think not thou canst sigh a sigh,
And thy Maker is not by;   30
Think not thou canst weep a tear,
And thy Maker is not near.

O! he gives to us his joy
That our grief he may destroy;
Till our grief is fled and gone,   35
He doth sit by us and moan.

SONGS OF EXPERIENCE

The Clod and the Pebble

'Love seeketh not itself to please,
Nor for itself hath any care,
But for another gives its ease,
And builds a Heaven in Hell's despair.'

So sang a little clod of clay,   5
Trodden with the cattle's feet;
But a pebble of the brook
Warbled out these metres meet:

'Love seeketh only self to please,
To bind another to its delight,   10
Joys in another's loss of ease,
And builds a Hell in Heaven's despite.'

The Little Girl Lost

In futurity
I, prophetic, see
That the earth from sleep
(Grave the sentence deep)

Shall arise and seek   5
For her maker meek,
And the desert wild
Become a garden mild.

In the southern clime,
Where the summer's prime   10
Never fades away,
Lovely Lyca lay.

Seven summers old
Lovely Lyca told.
She had wandered long   15
Hearing wild birds' song.

'Sweet sleep, come to me
Underneath this tree;
Do father, mother weep,
"Where can Lyca sleep?"   20

'Lost in desert wild
Is your little child.
How can Lyca sleep
If her mother weep?

'If her heart does ache   25
Then let Lyca wake;
If my mother sleep,
Lyca shall not weep.

'Frowning, frowning night,
O'er this desert bright   30
Let thy moon arise,
While I close my eyes.'

Sleeping Lyca lay—
While the beasts of prey
Come from caverns deep,   35
Viewed the maid asleep.

The kingly lion stood
And the virgin viewed;
Then he gambolled round
O'er the hallowed ground.   40

Leopards, tigers play
Round her as she lay,
While the lion old,
Bowed his mane of gold,

And her bosom lick;   45
And upon her neck,
From his eyes of flame
Ruby tears there came;

While the lioness
Loosed her slender dress,   50
And naked they conveyed
To caves the sleeping maid.

The Little Girl Found

All the night in woe
Lyca's parents go
Over valleys deep,
While the deserts weep.

Tired and woe-begone,   5
Hoarse with making moan,
Arm in arm, seven days
They traced the desert ways.

Seven nights they sleep
Among shadows deep,   10
And dream they see their child
Starved in desert wild.

Pale, through pathless ways
The fancied image strays—
Famished, weeping, weak,   15
With hollow piteous shriek.

Rising from unrest
The trembling woman pressed,
With feet of weary woe;
She could not further go.   20

In his arms he bore
Her, armed with sorrow sore—
Till before their way
A couching lion lay.

Turning back was vain;   25
Soon his heavy mane
Bore them to the ground;
Then he stalked around,

Smelling to his prey.
But their fears allay   30
When he licks their hands;
And silent by them stands.

They look upon his eyes
Filled with deep surprise,
And wondering behold;   35
A spirit armed in gold;

On his head a crown,
On his shoulders down
Flowed his golden hair—
Gone was all their care.   40

'Follow me,' he said,
'Weep not for the maid;
In my palace deep
Lyca lies asleep.'

Then they followèd   45
Where the vision led,
And saw their sleeping child
Among tigers wild.

To this day they dwell
In a lonely dell,   50
Nor fear the wolvish howl
Nor the lion's growl.

The Tiger

Tiger, tiger, burning bright
In the forests of the night,
What immortal hand or eye
Could frame thy fearful symmetry?

In what distant deeps or skies   5
Burnt the fire of thine eyes?
On what wings dare he aspire?
What the hand dare seize the fire?

And what shoulder and what art
Could twist the sinews of thy heart?   10
And when thy heart began to beat,
What dread hand? And what dread feet?

What the hammer? What the chain?
In what furnace was thy brain?
What the anvil? What dread grasp   15
Dare its deadly terrors clasp?

When the stars threw down their spears
And watered Heaven with their tears,
Did he smile his work to see?
Did he who made the lamb make thee?   20

Tiger, tiger, burning bright
In the forests of the night,
What immortal hand or eye
Dare frame thy fearful symmetry?

London

I wander through each chartered street
Near where the chartered Thames does flow,
And mark in every face I meet
Marks of weakness, marks of woe.

In every cry of every man,   5
In every infant's cry of fear,
In every voice, in every ban,
The mind-forged manacles I hear—

How the chimney-sweeper's cry
Every black'ning church appals,   10
And the hapless soldier's sigh
Runs in blood down palace walls;

But most through midnight streets I hear
How the youthful harlot's curse
Blasts the new-born infant's tear,   15
And blights with plagues the marriage-hearse.

WILLIAM WORDSWORTH
1770–1850

Wordsworth was born and lived most of his life in the Lake District. After taking his degree at Cambridge, he went on a walking tour of France and Switzerland and visited France again the following year. France was then (1790 and 1791) in the turmoil of revolution and Wordsworth enthusiastically supported the Republicans. He fell in love with a Frenchwoman, Annette Vallon, who bore his child. But the war between England and France separated him from Annette and for the next few years he lived with his sister Dorothy in Somerset, not far from the village where the poet Coleridge was then living.

These years were the most productive and creative in his life. In 1798, he and Coleridge together published the *Lyrical Ballads*, which included the Lucy poems, and he began writing his great autobiographical poem, *The Prelude*. The next year he and Dorothy moved back to the Lake District and settled at Dove Cottage in Grasmere. In 1802 he married a childhood friend, Mary Hutchinson. The letters they exchanged whenever Wordsworth was away from home show how deep and lasting was their love for each other.

Many of Wordsworth's more famous poems are too long to be included here, but his major themes are represented. In poem after poem, Wordsworth broods on the relationship between man and nature, drawing on his own experience. He was, in his own words, 'a worshipper of nature' which was a source to him of both terror and strength as well as joy. His aim as a poet was to re-create in the reader's mind both the experience he had undergone and his subsequent emotional reaction to it. You will not find, in Wordsworth, many descriptions of particular scenes, for it is the emotional meaning which nature can have and not its visual impact which occupied him as man and poet.

Stylistically, Wordsworth wanted to avoid what he took to be the 'gaudiness and inane phraseology' of many of his contemporaries and predecessors. His aim, as he put it in the 1805 edition of the *Lyrical Ballads*, was 'to choose incidents and situations from common life, and to relate or describe them throughout, as far as was possible, in a selection of language really used by men.' The result is not a genuinely rustic language, but it is a natural language, untainted by 'gaudiness': the language of 'a man speaking to men'.

Nutting

It seems a day
(I speak of one from many singled out)
One of those heavenly days that cannot die;
When, in the eagerness of boyish hope,
I left our cottage-threshold, sallying forth   5
With a huge wallet o'er my shoulders slung,
A nutting-crook in hand; and turned my steps
Tow'rd some far-distant wood, a Figure quaint,
Tricked out in proud disguise of cast-off weeds
Which for that service had been husbanded,   10
By exhortation of my frugal Dame—
Motley accoutrement, of power to smile
At thorns, and brakes, and brambles,—and in truth
More ragged than need was! O'er pathless rocks,
Through beds of matted fern, and tangled thickets,   15

Forcing my way, I came to one dear nook
Unvisited, where not a broken bough
Drooped with its withered leaves, ungracious sign
Of devastation; but the hazels rose
Tall and erect, with tempting clusters hung,   20
A virgin scene!—A little while I stood,
Breathing with such suppression of the heart
As joy delights in; and with wise restraint
Voluptuous, fearless of a rival, eyed
The banquet;—or beneath the trees I sate   25
Among the flowers, and with the flowers I played;
A temper known to those who, after long
And weary expectation, have been blest
With sudden happiness beyond all hope.
Perhaps it was a bower beneath whose leaves   30
The violets of five seasons re-appear
And fade, unseen by any human eye;
Where fairy water-breaks do murmur on
For ever; and I saw the sparkling foam,
And—with my cheek on one of those green stones   35
That, fleeced with moss, under the shady trees,
Lay round me, scattered like a flock of sheep—
I heard the murmur and the murmuring sound,
In that sweet mood when pleasure loves to pay
Tribute to ease: and, of its joy secure,   40
The heart luxuriates with indifferent things,
Wasting its kindliness on stocks and stones,
And on the vacant air. Then up I rose,
And dragged to earth both branch and bough, with crash
And merciless ravage: and the shady nook   45
Of hazels, and the green and mossy bower,
Deformed and sullied, patiently gave up
Their quiet being: and unless I now
Confound my present feelings with the past,
Ere from the mutilated bower I turned   50
Exulting, rich beyond the wealth of kings,
I felt a sense of pain when I beheld
The silent trees, and saw the intruding sky.—
Then, dearest Maiden, move along these shades
In gentleness of heart; with gentle hand   55
Touch – for there is a spirit in the woods.

Lucy Poems

Strange fits of passion have I known:
And I will dare to tell,
But in the Lover's ear alone,
What once to me befell.

When she I loved looked every day   5
Fresh as a rose in June,
I to her cottage bent my way,
Beneath an evening-moon.

Upon the moon I fixed my eye,
All over the wide lea;   10
With quickening pace my horse drew nigh
Those paths so dear to me.

And now we reached the orchard-plot;
And, as we climbed the hill,
The sinking moon to Lucy's cot   15
Came near, and nearer still.

In one of those sweet dreams I slept,
Kind Nature's gentlest boon!
And all the while my eyes I kept
On the descending moon.   20

My horse moved on; hoof after hoof
He raised, and never stopped:
When down behind the cottage roof,
At once, the bright moon dropped.

What fond and wayward thoughts will slide   25
Into a Lover's head!
'O mercy!' to myself I cried,
'If Lucy should be dead!'

*   *   *

She dwelt among the untrodden ways
    Beside the springs of Dove,
A Maid whom there were none to praise
    And very few to love:

A violet by a mossy stone   5
    Half hidden from the eye!
Fair as a star, when only one
    Is shining in the sky.

She lived unknown, and few could know
    When Lucy ceased to be;   10
But she is in her grave, and oh,
    The difference to me!

*   *   *

I travelled among unknown men,
    In lands beyond the sea;
Nor, England! did I know till then
    What love I bore to thee.

'Tis past, that melancholy dream!   5
    Nor will I quit thy shore
A second time; for still I seem
    To love thee more and more.

Among thy mountains did I feel
    The joy of my desire;   10
And she I cherished turned her wheel
    Beside an English fire.

Thy mornings showed, thy nights concealed,
    The bowers where Lucy played;
And thine too is the last green field   15
    That Lucy's eyes surveyed.

*   *   *

A slumber did my spirit seal;
   I had no human fears:
She seemed a thing that could not feel
   The touch of earthly years.

No motion has she now, no force;   5
   She neither hears nor sees;
Rolled round in earth's diurnal course,
   With rocks, and stones, and trees.

Upon Westminster Bridge, September 3, 1802

Earth has not anything to show more fair:
Dull would he be of soul who could pass by
A sight so touching in its majesty:
This City now doth, like a garment, wear
The beauty of the morning; silent, bare,   5
Ships, towers, domes, theatres, and temples lie
Open unto the fields, and to the sky;
All bright and glittering in the smokeless air.
Never did sun more beautifully steep
In his first splendour, valley, rock, or hill;   10
Ne'er saw I, never felt, a calm so deep!
The river glideth at his own sweet will:
Dear God! the very houses seem asleep;
And all that mighty heart is lying still!

Resolution and Independence

I

There was a roaring in the wind all night;
The rain came heavily and fell in floods;
But now the sun is rising calm and bright;
The birds are singing in the distant woods;
Over his own sweet voice the stock-dove broods;   5
The jay makes answer as the magpie chatters;
And all the air is filled with pleasant noise of waters.

II

All things that love the sun are out of doors;
The sky rejoices in the morning's birth;
The grass is bright with rain-drops,—on the moors   10
The hare is running races in her mirth;
And with her feet she from the plashy earth
Raises a mist; that, glittering in the sun,
Runs with her all the way, wherever she doth run.

III

I was a Traveller then upon the moor;   15
I saw the hare that raced about with joy;
I heard the woods and distant waters roar;
Or heard them not, as happy as a boy:
The pleasant season did my heart employ:
My old remembrances went from me wholly;   20
And all the ways of men, so vain and melancholy.

IV

But, as it sometimes chanceth, from the might
Of joy in minds that can no further go,
As high as we have mounted in delight
In our dejection do we sink as low;   25
To me that morning did it happen so;
And fears and fancies thick upon me came;
Dim sadness—and blind thoughts, I knew not, nor could name.

V

I heard the sky-lark warbling in the sky;
And I bethought me of the playful hare: 30
Even such a happy Child of earth am I;
Even as these blissful creatures do I fare;
Far from the world I walk, and from all care;
But there may come another day to me—
Solitude, pain of heart, distress, and poverty. 35

VI

My whole life I have lived in pleasant thought,
As if life's business were a summer mood;
As if all needful things would come unsought
To genial faith, still rich in genial good;
But how can he expect that others should 40
Build for him, sow for him, and at his call
Love him, who for himself will take no heed at all?

VII

I thought of Chatterton, the marvellous Boy,
The sleepless Soul that perished in his pride;
Of Him who walked in glory and in joy 45
Following his plough, along the mountain-side:
By our own spirits are we deified:
We Poets in our youth begin in gladness;
But thereof come in the end despondency and madness.

VIII

Now, whether it were by peculiar grace, 50
A leading from above, a something given,
Yet it befell that, in this lonely place,
When I with these untoward thoughts had striven,
Beside a pool bare to the eye of heaven
I saw a Man before me unawares: 55
The oldest man he seemed that ever wore grey hairs.

IX

As a huge stone is sometimes seen to lie
Couched on the bald top of an eminence;
Wonder to all who do the same espy,
By what means it could thither come, and whence; 60

So that it seems a thing endued with sense:
Like a sea-beast crawled forth, that on a shelf
Of rock or sand reposeth, there to sun itself;

    X
Such seemed this Man, not all alive nor dead,
Nor all asleep—in his extreme old age: 65
His body was bent double, feet and head
Coming together in life's pilgrimage;
As if some dire constraint of pain, or rage
Of sickness felt by him in times long past,
A more than human weight upon his frame had cast.   70

    XI
Himself he propped, limbs, body, and pale face,
Upon a long grey staff of shaven wood:
And, still as I drew near with gentle pace,
Upon the margin of that moorish flood
Motionless as a cloud the old Man stood,   75
That heareth not the loud winds when they call;
And moveth all together, if it move at all.

    XII
At length, himself unsettling, he the pond
Stirred with his staff, and fixedly did look
Upon the muddy water, which he conned,   80
As if he had been reading in a book:
And now a stranger's privilege I took;
And, drawing to his side, to him did say,
'This morning gives us promise of a glorious day'.

    XIII
A gentle answer did the old Man make,   85
In courteous speech which forth he slowly drew:
And him with further words I thus bespake,
'What occupation do you there pursue?
This is a lonesome place for one like you.'
Ere he replied, a flash of mild surprise   90
Broke from the sable orbs of his yet-vivid eyes.

XIV

His words came feebly, from a feeble chest,
But each in solemn order followed each,
With something of a lofty utterance drest—
Choice word and measured phrase, above the reach   95
Of ordinary men; a stately speech;
Such as grave Livers do in Scotland use,
Religious men, who give to God and man their dues.

XV

He told, that to these waters he had come
To gather leeches, being old and poor: 100
Employment hazardous and wearisome!
And he had many hardships to endure:
From pond to pond he roamed, from moor to moor;
Housing, with God's good help, by choice or chance;
And in this way he gained an honest maintenance.   105

XVI

The old Man still stood talking by my side;
But now his voice to me was like a stream
Scarce heard; nor word from word could I divide;
And the whole body of the Man did seem
Like one whom I had met with in a dream;   110
Or like a man from some far region sent,
To give me human strength, by apt admonishment.

XVII

My former thoughts returned: the fear that kills;
And hope that is unwilling to be fed;
Cold, pain, and labour, and all fleshly ills;   115
And mighty Poets in their misery dead.
—Perplexed, and longing to be comforted,
My question eagerly did I renew,
'How is it that you live, and what is it you do?'

XVIII

He with a smile did then his words repeat;   120
And said that, gathering leeches, far and wide
He travelled; stirring thus about his feet
The waters of the pools where they abide.

'Once I could meet with them on every side;
But they have dwindled long by slow decay;   125
Yet still I persevere, and find them where I may.'

    XIX
While he was talking thus, the lonely place,
The old Man's shape, and speech—all troubled me:
In my mind's eye I seemed to see him pace
About the weary moors continually,   130
Wandering about alone and silently.
While I these thoughts within myself pursued,
He, having made a pause, the same discourse renewed.

    XX
And soon with this he other matter blended,
Cheerfully uttered, with demeanour kind,   135
But stately in the main; and, when he ended,
I could have laughed myself to scorn to find
In that decrepit Man so firm a mind.
'God,' said I, 'be my help and stay secure;
I'll think of the Leech-gatherer on the lonely moor!'   140

I wandered lonely as a cloud

I wandered lonely as a cloud
That floats on high o'er vales and hills,
When all at once I saw a crowd,
A host, of golden daffodils;
Beside the lake, beneath the trees,   5
Fluttering and dancing in the breeze.

Continuous as the stars that shine
And twinkle on the Milky Way,
They stretched in never-ending line
Along the margin of a bay: 10
Ten thousand saw I at a glance,
Tossing their heads in sprightly dance.

The waves beside them danced, but they
Out-did the sparkling waves in glee:
A poet could not but be gay,   15
In such a jocund company:
I gazed—and gazed—but little thought
What wealth the show to me had brought:

For oft, when on my couch I lie
In vacant or in pensive mood,   20
They flash upon that inward eye
Which is the bliss of solitude;
And then my heart with pleasure fills,
And dances with the daffodils.

JOHN KEATS
1795–1821

Keats had an unsettled childhood. His father died when he was only nine, his mother re-married soon afterwards, and he and his two younger brothers went to live with their grandmother in north London. At 16, Keats was apprenticed to a surgeon, but though he qualified four years later, he decided to give up medicine so that he could devote his time to writing.

Most of his major poems, including the *Ode to a Nightingale, To Autumn* and the richly descriptive long narrative poem, *The Eve of St Agnes* were written in a few months in 1819. By then Keats was already suffering from consumption which he contracted after a strenuous walking tour of the Lake District and Scotland. He had returned to London with a sore throat and nursed his brother Tom till his death of the same disease. On his doctor's advice Keats sailed for Italy in the autumn of 1820, but he died a few months after arriving in Rome. He was 25.

Keats's working life as a poet lasted little more than five years.

Nevertheless, he managed, despite shortage of money, Tom's death and his own bad health, to publish three volumes of poetry. He also wrote long letters, describing his travels, his feelings and thoughts to his brothers, his friends, and to Fanny Brawne the girl whom he loved. She was his next door neighbour when he lodged in Hampstead and she and her mother nursed him before he left for Italy.

'Verbal magic', sensuous imagery and beauty of sound are typical of Keats's poetry. You tend, as Wilson Knight puts it, 'to touch, to smell, to taste, to feel the living warmth of one object after another'. Other critics have doubted whether anything very significant underlies this 'exquisite sense of the luxurious'. Some consider that Keats's 'yearning passion for the beautiful', as he himself described it, led him to write poems of fantasy and escape. Is *La Belle Dame Sans Merci* anything more than a haunting fairy tale? Or does the poem explore emotions which are meaningful and real? Is the *Ode to a Nightingale* a poem written to escape from 'the weariness, the fever and the fret' of a world 'where but to think is to be full of sorrow', or does Keats reject the idea of an 'easeful death'? In many of his poems a tremendous struggle seems to be taking place between a sense of luxurious beauty and a quest for truth.

On First Looking into Chapman's Homer

Much have I travelled in the realms of gold,
   And many goodly states and kingdoms seen;
   Round many western islands have I been
Which bards in fealty to Apollo hold.
Oft of one wide expanse had I been told   5
   That deep-browed Homer ruled as his demesne:
   Yet did I never breathe its pure serene
Till I heard Chapman speak out loud and bold:
Then felt I like some watcher of the skies
   When a new planet swims into his ken;   10
Or like stout Cortez, when with eagle eyes
   He stared at the Pacific—and all his men
Looked at each other with a wild surmise—
   Silent, upon a peak in Darien.

On the Sea

It keeps eternal whisperings around
   Desolate shores, and with its mighty swell
   Gluts twice ten thousand caverns; till the spell
Of Hecate leaves them their old shadowy sound.
Often 'tis in such gentle temper found   5
   That scarcely will the very smallest shell
   Be moved for days from whence it sometime fell,
When last the winds of heaven were unbound.
O ye who have your eyeballs vext and tired,
   Feast them upon the wideness of the sea;   10
     O ye whose ears are dinned with uproar rude,
   Or fed too much with cloying melody—
     Sit ye near some old cavern's mouth and brood
Until ye start, as if the sea nymphs quired.

La Belle Dame Sans Merci

'O what can ail thee, knight-at-arms,
   Alone and palely loitering?
The sedge has withered from the lake,
   And no birds sing.

'O what can ail thee, knight-at-arms,   5
   So haggard and so woe-begone?
The squirrel's granary is full,
   And the harvest's done.

'I see a lily on thy brow
   With anguish moist and fever dew;   10
And on thy cheek a fading rose
   Fast withereth too.'

'I met a lady in the meads,
   Full beautiful – a faery's child,
Her hair was long, her foot was light,   15
   And her eyes were wild.

'I made a garland for her head,
   And bracelets too, and fragrant zone;
She looked at me as she did love,
   And made sweet moan.   20

'I set her on my pacing steed
   And nothing else saw all day long,
For sideways would she lean, and sing
   A faery's song.

'She found me roots of relish sweet,   25
   And honey wild and manna dew,
And sure in language strange she said,
   "I love thee true!"

'She took me to her elfin grot,
   And there she wept and sighed full sore;   30
And there I shut her wild, wild eyes
   With kisses four.

'And there she lullèd me asleep,
   And there I dreamed – Ah! woe betide!
The latest dream I ever dreamed   35
   On the cold hill's side.

'I saw pale kings and princes too,
   Pale warriors, death-pale were they all;
Who cried – "La Belle Dame sans Merci
   Hath thee in thrall!"   40

'I saw their starved lips in the gloam
   With horrid warning gapèd wide,
And I awoke and found me here
   On the cold hill's side.

'And this is why I sojourn here   45
   Alone and palely loitering,
Though the sedge is withered from the lake,
   And no birds sing.'

Ode to a Nightingale

My heart aches, and a drowsy numbness pains
   My sense, as though of hemlock I had drunk,
Or emptied some dull opiate to the drains
   One minute past, and Lethe-wards had sunk:
'Tis not through envy of thy happy lot,   5
   But being too happy in thy happiness,
      That thou, light-wingèd Dryad of the trees,
         In some melodious plot
   Of beechen green, and shadows numberless,
      Singest of summer in full-throated ease.   10

O for a draught of vintage! that hath been
   Cooled a long age in the deep-delvèd earth,
Tasting of Flora and the country-green,
   Dance, and Provençal song, and sunburnt mirth!
O for a beaker full of the warm South!   15
   Full of the true, the blushful Hippocrene,
      With beaded bubbles winking at the brim,
         And purple-stainèd mouth;
   That I might drink, and leave the world unseen,
      And with thee fade away into the forest dim: 20

Fade far away, dissolve, and quite forget
   What thou among the leaves hast never known,
The weariness, the fever, and the fret
   Here, where men sit and hear each other groan;
Where palsy shakes a few, sad, last grey hairs,   25
   Where youth grows pale, and spectre-thin, and dies;
      Where but to think is to be full of sorrow
         And leaden-eyed despairs;
   Where Beauty cannot keep her lustrous eyes,
      Or new Love pine at them beyond to-morrow.   30

Away! away! for I will fly to thee,
   Not charioted by Bacchus and his pards,
But on the viewless wings of Poesy,
   Though the dull brain perplexes and retards:
Already with thee! tender is the night,   35

And haply the Queen-Moon is on her throne,
  Clustered around by all her starry Fays;
      But here there is no light,
  Save what from heaven is with the breezes blown
    Through verdurous glooms and winding mossy ways.   40

I cannot see what flowers are at my feet,
  Nor what soft incense hangs upon the boughs,
But, in embalmèd darkness, guess each sweet
  Wherewith the seasonable month endows
The grass, the thicket, and the fruit-tree wild;   45
  White hawthorn, and the pastoral eglantine;
    Fast fading violets covered up in leaves;
        And mid-May's eldest child,
  The coming musk-rose, full of dewy wine,
    The murmurous haunt of flies on summer eves.   50

Darkling I listen; and for many a time
  I have been half in love with easeful Death,
Called him soft names in many a musèd rhyme,
  To take into the air my quiet breath;
Now more than ever seems it rich to die,   55
  To cease upon the midnight with no pain,
    While thou art pouring forth thy soul abroad
        In such an ecstasy!
  Still wouldst thou sing, and I have ears in vain—
    To thy high requiem become a sod.   60

Thou wast not born for death, immortal Bird!
  No hungry generations tread thee down;
The voice I hear this passing night was heard
  In ancient days by emperor and clown:
Perhaps the self-same song that found a path   65
  Through the sad heart of Ruth, when, sick for home,
    She stood in tears amid the alien corn;
        The same that oft times hath
  Charmed magic casements, opening on the foam
    Of perilous seas, in faery lands forlorn.   70

Forlorn! the very word is like a bell
  To toll me back from thee to my sole self!

Adieu! the fancy cannot cheat so well
   As she is famed to do, deceiving elf.
Adieu! adieu! thy plaintive anthem fades   75
   Past the near meadows, over the still stream,
     Up the hill-side; and now 'tis buried deep
        In the next valley-glades:
   Was it a vision, or a waking dream?
   Fled is that music: – do I wake or sleep?   80

To Autumn

Season of mists and mellow fruitfulness!
   Close bosom-friend of the maturing sun;
Conspiring with him how to load and bless
   With fruit the vines that round the thatch-eaves run;
To bend with apples the mossed cottage-trees,   5
   And fill all fruit with ripeness to the core;
     To swell the gourd, and plump the hazel shells
With a sweet kernel; to set budding more,
   And still more, later flowers for the bees,
     Until they think warm days will never cease,   10
      For Summer has o'erbrimmed their clammy cells.

Who hath not seen thee oft amid thy store?
   Sometimes whoever seeks abroad may find
Thee sitting careless on a granary floor,
   Thy hair soft-lifted by the winnowing wind,   15
Or on a half-reaped furrow sound asleep,
   Drowsed with the fume of poppies, while thy hook
     Spares the next swath and all its twinèd flowers;
And sometimes like a gleaner thou dost keep
   Steady thy laden head across a brook;   20
   Or by a cider-press, with patient look,
     Thou watchest the last oozings hours by hours.

Where are the songs of Spring? Ay, where are they?
　Think not of them, thou hast thy music too,—
While barred clouds bloom the soft-dying day,　　25
　And touch the stubble-plains with rosy hue;
Then in a wailful choir the small gnats mourn
　Among the river sallows, borne aloft
　　Or sinking as the light wind lives or dies;
And full-grown lambs loud bleat from hilly bourn;　　30
　Hedge-crickets sing; and now with treble soft
　The redbreast whistles from a garden-croft;
　　And gathering swallows twitter in the skies.

Last Sonnet

Bright star, would I were steadfast as thou art—
　Not in lone splendour hung aloft the night,
And watching, with eternal lids apart,
　Like Nature's patient sleepless Eremite,
The moving waters at their priest-like task　　5
　Of pure ablution round earth's human shores,
Or gazing on the new soft-fallen mask
　Of snow upon the mountains and the moors—
No—yet still steadfast, still unchangeable,
　Pillowed upon my fair love's ripening breast,　　10
To feel for ever its soft fall and swell,
　Awake for ever in a sweet unrest,
　　Still, still to hear her tender-taken breath,
　　And so live ever—or else swoon to death.

ALFRED, LORD TENNYSON
1809–1892

Alfred Tennyson was born at Somersby, a village in Lincolnshire where his father was rector. He was the fourth child in a large family of twelve children and from his childhood years he preferred to spend his time in solitude, shyly secluded from the rest of the family, reading poetry. Sometimes his father, who was prone to fits of anger and dark despair, drove the young Tennyson out into the churchyard where he would fight with his own bleak feelings.

Tennyson wrote his first poem when he was eight years old. He was educated at a local grammar school and at home before going to Cambridge University in 1828. At University he was one of a circle of fashionable young poets and writers. He made a particular friend of Arthur Hallam with whom he went on holidays, walking and sight-seeing in the Pyrenees and along the river Rhine in Germany. Hallam came to know the Tennysons well and was engaged to Tennyson's sister Emily. When his father died in 1830, Tennyson returned home without taking his degree and published his first book, *Poems, Chiefly Lyrical*. *Mariana* is taken from this volume.

In 1832 *The Lady of Shalott and Other Poems* was viciously attacked by critics whose comments wounded the nervous and sensitive young poet. More seriously, in 1833, on a trip to Vienna, Arthur Hallam died of a brain haemorrhage aged only 22. This was the most important event in Tennyson's life. His sister suffered a nervous breakdown, while Tennyson, stunned and shocked by the death of his friend, took the next twenty years to come to terms with his grief. It was ten years before he published his next collection of verse. His most famous poem, *In Memoriam*, in which he attempted to express the feelings of loneliness and despair with which he had been struggling since Hallam's death, appeared in 1850. In the same year Tennyson married Emily Sellwood, to whom he had been engaged for fourteen years, and was appointed Poet Laureate, after Wordsworth.

For the next forty years of his life, Tennyson continued to write poetry. He received considerable public acclaim and became a personal friend of Queen Victoria. Many people have nevertheless thought that his poetical gifts declined after the publication of *In Memoriam*. As a later Poet Laureate, Alfred Austin, put it: 'his fame . . . increased precisely as his genuine poetical power . . . steadily waned'.

Mariana

'Mariana in the moated grange'
Measure for Measure

With blackest moss the flower-pots
   Were thickly crusted, one and all:
The rusted nails fell from the knots
   That held the pear to the gable-wall.
The broken sheds looked sad and strange: 5
   Unlifted was the clinking latch;
   Weeded and worn the ancient thatch
Upon the lonely moated grange.
     She only said, 'My life is dreary,
       He cometh not,' she said;   10
     She said, 'I am aweary, aweary,
       I would that I were dead!'

Her tears fell with the dews at even;
   Her tears fell ere the dews were dried;
She could not look on the sweet heaven,   15
   Either at morn or eventide.
After the flitting of the bats,
   When thickest dark did trance the sky,
   She drew her casement-curtain by,
And glanced athwart the glooming flats.   20
      She only said, 'The night is dreary,
         He cometh not,' she said;
      She said, 'I am aweary, aweary,
         I would that I were dead!'

Upon the middle of the night,   25
   Waking she heard the night-fowl crow:
The cock sung out an hour ere light:
   From the dark fen the oxen's low
Came to her: without hope of change,
   In sleep she seemed to walk forlorn,   30
   Till cold winds woke the gray-eyed morn
About the lonely moated grange.
      She only said, 'The day is dreary,
         He cometh not,' she said;
      She said, 'I am aweary, aweary,   35
         I would that I were dead!'

About a stone-cast from the wall
   A sluice with blackened waters slept,
And o'er it many, round and small,
   The clustered marish-mosses crept.   40
Hard by a poplar shook alway,
   All silver-green with gnarlèd bark:
   For leagues no other tree did mark
The level waste, the rounding gray.
      She only said, 'My life is dreary,   45
         He cometh not,' she said;
      She said, 'I am aweary, aweary,
         I would that I were dead!'

And ever when the moon was low,
   And the shrill winds were up and away,   50
In the white curtain, to and fro,
   She saw the gusty shadow sway.
But when the moon was very low,
   And wild winds bound within their cell,
   The shadow of the poplar fell   55
Upon her bed, across her brow.
     She only said, 'The night is dreary,
      He cometh not,' she said;
     She said, 'I am aweary, aweary,
      I would that I were dead!'   60

All day within the dreamy house,
   The doors upon their hinges creaked;
The blue fly sung in the pane; the mouse
   Behind the mouldering wainscot shrieked,
Or from the crevice peered about.   65
   Old faces glimmered through the doors,
   Old footsteps trod the upper floors,
Old voices called her from without.
     She only said, 'My life is dreary,
      He cometh not,' she said;   70
     She said, 'I am aweary, aweary,
      I would that I were dead!'

The sparrow's chirrup on the roof,
   The slow clock ticking, and the sound
Which to the wooing wind aloof   75
   The poplar made, did all confound
Her sense; but most she loathed the hour
   When the thick-moted sunbeam lay
   Athwart the chambers, and the day
Was sloping toward his western bower.   80
     Then, said she, 'I am very dreary,
      He will not come,' she said;
     She wept, 'I am aweary, aweary,
      Oh God, that I were dead!'

The Lady of Shalott

PART I

On either side the river lie
Long fields of barley and of rye,
That clothe the wold and meet the sky;
And through the field the road runs by
  To many-towered Camelot;   5
And up and down the people go,
Gazing where the lilies blow
Round an island there below,
  The island of Shalott.

Willows whiten, aspens quiver,   10
Little breezes dusk and shiver
Through the wave that runs for ever
By the island in the river
  Flowing down to Camelot.
Four gray walls, and four gray towers, 15
Overlook a space of flowers,
And the silent isle imbowers
  The Lady of Shalott.

By the margin, willow-veiled,
Slide the heavy barges trailed   20
By slow horses; and unhailed
The shallop flitteth silken-sailed
  Skimming down to Camelot:
But who hath seen her wave her hand?
Or at the casement seen her stand? 25
Or is she known in all the land,
  The Lady of Shalott?

Only reapers, reaping early
In among the bearded barley,
Hear a song that echoes cheerly   30
From the river winding clearly,
  Down to towered Camelot:

And by the moon the reaper weary,
Piling sheaves in uplands airy,
Listening, whispers ' 'Tis the fairy   35
    Lady of Shalott.'

    PART II
There she weaves by night and day
A magic web with colours gay.
She has heard a whisper say,
A curse is on her if she stay   40
    To look down to Camelot.
She knows not what the curse may be,
And so she weaveth steadily,
And little other care hath she,
    The Lady of Shalott.   45

And moving through a mirror clear
That hangs before her all the year,
Shadows of the world appear.
There she sees the highway near
    Winding down to Camelot: 50
There the river eddy whirls,
And there the surly village-churls,
And the red cloaks of market girls,
    Pass onward from Shalott.

Sometimes a troop of damsels glad,   55
An abbot on an ambling pad,
Sometimes a curly shepherd-lad,
Or long-haired page in crimson clad,
    Goes by to towered Camelot;
And sometimes through the mirror blue   60
The knights come riding two and two:
She hath no loyal knight and true,
    The Lady of Shalott.

But in her web she still delights
To weave the mirror's magic sights,   65
For often through the silent nights
A funeral, with plumes and lights
    And music, went to Camelot:

Or when the moon was overhead,
Came two young lovers lately wed;   70
'I am half sick of shadows,' said
    The Lady of Shalott.

    PART III
A bow-shot from her bower-eaves,
He rode between the barley-sheaves,
The sun came dazzling through the leaves,   75
And flamed upon the brazen greaves
    Of bold Sir Lancelot.
A red-cross knight for ever kneeled
To a lady in his shield,
That sparkled on the yellow field,   80
    Beside remote Shalott.

The gemmy bridle glittered free,
Like to some branch of stars we see
Hung in the golden Galaxy.
The bridle bells rang merrily   85
    As he rode down to Camelot:
And from his blazoned baldric slung
A mighty silver bugle hung,
And as he rode his armour rung,
    Beside remote Shalott.   90

All in the blue unclouded weather
Thick-jewelled shone the saddle-leather,
The helmet and the helmet-feather
Burned like one burning flame together,
    As he rode down to Camelot.   95
As often through the purple night,
Below the starry clusters bright,
Some bearded meteor, trailing light,
    Moves over still Shalott.

His broad clear brow in sunlight glowed;   100
On burnished hooves his war-horse trode;
From underneath his helmet flowed
His coal-black curls as on he rode,
    As he rode down to Camelot.

From the bank and from the river   105
He flashed into the crystal mirror,
'Tirra lirra,' by the river
    Sang Sir Lancelot.

She left the web, she left the loom,
She made three paces through the room,   110
She saw the water-lily bloom,
She saw the helmet and the plume,
    She looked down to Camelot.
Out flew the web and floated wide;
The mirror cracked from side to side;   115
'The curse is come upon me,' cried
    The Lady of Shalott.

PART IV

In the stormy east-wind straining,
The pale yellow woods were waning,
The broad stream in his banks complaining, 120
Heavily the low sky raining
    Over towered Camelot;
Down she came and found a boat
Beneath a willow left afloat,
And round about the prow she wrote   125
    The Lady of Shalott.

And down the river's dim expanse
Like some bold seër in a trance,
Seeing all his own mischance—
With a glassy countenance   130
    Did she look to Camelot.
And at the closing of the day
She loosed the chain, and down she lay;
The broad stream bore her far away,
    The Lady of Shalott.   135

Lying, robed in snowy white
That loosely flew to left and right—
The leaves upon her falling light—
Through the noises of the night
    She floated down to Camelot: 140

And as the boat-head wound along
The willowy hills and fields among,
They heard her singing her last song,
    The Lady of Shalott.

Heard a carol, mournful, holy,   145
Chanted loudly, chanted slowly,
Till her blood was frozen slowly,
And her eyes were darkened wholly,
    Turned to towered Camelot.
For ere she reached upon the tide   150
The first house by the water-side,
Singing in her song she died,
    The Lady of Shalott.

Under tower and balcony,
By garden-wall and gallery,   155
A gleaming shape she floated by,
Dead-pale between the houses high,
    Silent into Camelot.
Out upon the wharfs they came,
Knight and burgher, lord and dame,   160
And round the prow they read her name,
    The Lady of Shalott.

Who is this? and what is here?
And in the lighted palace near
Died the sound of royal cheer;   165
And they crossed themselves for fear,
    All the knights at Camelot:
But Lancelot mused a little space;
He said, 'She has a lovely face;
God in his mercy lend her grace,   170
    The Lady of Shalott.'

Ulysses

It little profits that an idle king,
By this still hearth, among these barren crags,
Matched with an agèd wife, I mete and dole
Unequal laws unto a savage race,
That hoard, and sleep, and feed, and know not me.   5

   I cannot rest from travel: I will drink
Life to the lees: all times I have enjoyed
Greatly, have suffered greatly, both with those
That loved me, and alone; on shore, and when
Through scudding drifts the rainy Hyades   10
Vext the dim sea: I am become a name;
For always roaming with a hungry heart
Much have I seen and known; cities of men
And manners, climates, councils, governments,
Myself not least, but honoured of them all;   15
And drunk delight of battle with my peers,
Far on the ringing plains of windy Troy.

   I am a part of all that I have met;
Yet all experience is an arch wherethrough
Gleams that untravelled world, whose margin fades   20
For ever and for ever when I move.
How dull it is to pause, to make an end,
To rust unburnished, not to shine in use!
As though to breathe were life. Life piled on life
Were all too little, and of one to me   25
Little remains: but every hour is saved
From that eternal silence, something more,
A bringer of new things; and vile it were
For some three suns to store and hoard myself,
And this gray spirit yearning in desire   30
To follow knowledge like a sinking star,
Beyond the utmost bound of human thought.

   This is my son, mine own Telemachus,
To whom I leave the sceptre and the isle—
Well-loved of me, discerning to fulfil   35

This labour, by slow prudence to make mild
A rugged people, and through soft degrees
Subdue them to the useful and the good.
Most blameless is he, centred in the sphere
Of common duties, decent not to fail   40
In offices of tenderness, and pay
Meet adoration to my household gods,
When I am gone. He works his work, I mine.

    There lies the port; the vessel puffs her sail:
There gloom the dark broad seas. My mariners,   45
Souls that have toiled, and wrought, and thought with me—
That ever with a frolic welcome took
The thunder and the sunshine, and opposed
Free hearts, free foreheads—you and I are old;
Old age hath yet his honour and his toil;   50
Death closes all: but something ere the end,
Some work of noble note, may yet be done,
Not unbecoming men that strove with Gods.
The lights begin to twinkle from the rocks:
The long day wanes: the slow moon climbs: the deep   55
Moans round with many voices. Come, my friends,
'Tis not too late to seek a newer world.
Push off, and sitting well in order smite
The sounding furrows; for my purpose holds
To sail beyond the sunset, and the baths   60
Of all the western stars, until I die.
It may be that the gulfs will wash us down:
It may be we shall touch the Happy Isles,
And see the great Achilles, whom we knew.
Though much is taken, much abides; and though   65
We are not now that strength which in old days
Moved earth and heaven; that which we are, we are;
One equal temper of heroic hearts,
Made weak by time and fate, but strong in will
To strive, to seek, to find, and not to yield.   70

from In Memoriam

Dark house, by which once more I stand
   Here in the long unlovely street,
   Doors, where my heart was used to beat
So quickly, waiting for a hand,

A hand that can be clasped no more—   5
   Behold me, for I cannot sleep,
   And like a guilty thing I creep
At earliest morning to the door.

He is not here; but far away
   The noise of life begins again,   10
   And ghastly through the drizzling rain
On the bald street breaks the blank day.

*   *   *

With trembling fingers did we weave
   The holly round the Christmas hearth;
   A rainy cloud possessed the earth,
And sadly fell our Christmas-eve.

At our old pastimes in the hall   5
   We gambolled, making vain pretence
   Of gladness, with an awful sense
Of one mute Shadow watching all.

We paused: the winds were in the beech:
   We heard them sweep the winter land;   10
   And in a circle hand-in-hand
Sat silent, looking each at each.

Then echo-like our voices rang;
   We sung, though every eye was dim,
   A merry song we sang with him   15
Last year: impetuously we sang:

We ceased: a gentler feeling crept
   Upon us: surely rest is meet:
   'They rest,' we said, 'their sleep is sweet,'
And silence followed, and we wept.   20

Our voices took a higher range;
   Once more we sang: 'They do not die
   Nor lose their mortal sympathy,
Nor change to us, although they change;

'Rapt from the fickle and the frail   25
   With gathered power, yet the same,
   Pierces the keen seraphic flame
From orb to orb, from veil to veil.'

Rise, happy morn, rise, holy morn,
   Draw forth the cheerful day from night: 30
   O Father, touch the east, and light
The light that shone when Hope was born.

*   *   *

Again at Christmas did we weave
   The holly round the Christmas hearth;
   The silent snow possessed the earth,
And calmly fell our Christmas-eve:

The yule-log sparkled keen with frost,   5
   No wing of wind the region swept,
   But over all things brooding slept
The quiet sense of something lost.

As in the winters left behind,
   Again our ancient games had place,   10
   The mimic picture's breathing grace,
And dance and song and hoodman-blind.

Who showed a token of distress?
    No single tear, no mark of pain:
    O sorrow, then can sorrow wane?   15
O grief, can grief be changed to less?

O last regret, regret can die!
    No – mixt with all this mystic frame,
    Her deep relations are the same,
But with long use her tears are dry.   20

ROBERT BROWNING
1812–1889

Robert Browning was born in London in 1812. His father was a
wealthy bank employee who encouraged his son to write, support-
ing him for many years with a private income. In 1846 Browning
married the poet Elizabeth Barrett and eloped with her to Italy. She
died fifteen years later and he returned to live in England where he
continued to publish a great number of poems and plays. His best
poetry was written, however, in the years which he spent in Italy
with his wife.

Many of Browning's most interesting poems are 'dramatic
monologues'. A dramatic monologue is a poem in which a single
character is either speaking to an imaginary listener (as in *A Light
Woman* or *My Last Duchess*) or to himself (as in *Porphyria's Lover*). The
characters who speak in Browning's monologues are often men and
women caught at moments of anxiety and obsession. Since they
tend to reveal more than they actually intend, the interest of these
poems lies in discovering what lies beneath the words which are

actually spoken. How, for instance, has the Duke's first wife died in *My Last Duchess*, and how should we as readers (or 'listeners') respond to the personality which is gradually revealed to us as he speaks? What is the truth of the speaker's relationship with the 'light woman' in the poem of that title? As you read the poems which follow you will be faced with psychological and moral problems of this kind.

Many of Browning's poems reflect his interest in music, painting and religion. It is, however, as a love poet, and as a love poet who was acutely aware of how men and women can be separated by jealousy or the passing of time, that he is often remembered. Failed relationships of one kind or another lie behind the dramatic monologues already mentioned. *Meeting at Night* dramatizes the excitement and intensity of passion, but *Parting at Morning* recognizes the complexities which morning inevitably brings. 'I would I could adopt your will,/See with your eyes, and set my heart/Beating by yours' he writes to his loved one in *Two in the Campagna*. The lines with which this poem ends:

> Only I discern –
> Infinite passion, and the pain
> Of finite hearts that yearn.

show that Browning fully faced the sad complexity of many human relationships, but he often expressed the positive, joyful side of love and friendship too.

Meeting at Night

The grey sea and the long black land;
And the yellow half-moon large and low;
And the startled little waves that leap
In fiery ringlets from their sleep,
As I gain the cove with pushing prow,   5
And quench its speed in the slushy sand.

Then a mile of warm sea-scented beach;
Three fields to cross till a farm appears;
A tap at the pane, the quick sharp scratch
And blue spurt of a lighted match,   10
And a voice less loud, through its joys and fears,
Than the two hearts beating each to each!

Parting at Morning

Round the cape of a sudden came the sea,
And the sun looked over the mountain's rim:
And straight was a path of gold for him,
And the need of a world of men for me.

A Light Woman

So far as our story approaches the end,   1
    Which do you pity the most of us three?—
My friend, or the mistress of my friend
    With her wanton eyes, or me?

My friend was already too good to lose,   5
    And seemed in the way of improvement yet,
When she crossed his path with her hunting-noose
    And over him drew her net.

When I saw him tangled in her toils,
    A shame, said I, if she adds just him   10
To her nine-and-ninety other spoils,
    The hundredth, for a whim!

And before my friend be wholly hers,
    How easy to prove to him, I said,
An eagle's the game her pride prefers,   15
    Though she snaps at a wren instead!

So I gave her eyes my own eyes to take,
   My hand sought hers as in earnest need,
And round she turned for my noble sake,
   And gave me herself indeed.   20

The eagle am I, with my fame in the world,
   The wren is he, with his maiden face.
—You look away and your lip is curled?
   Patience, a moment's space!

For see—my friend goes shaking and white;   25
   He eyes me as the basilisk:
I have turned, it appears, his day to night,
   Eclipsing his sun's disk.

And I did it, he thinks, as a very thief:
   'Though I love her—that, he comprehends—   30
One should master one's passions, (love, in chief)
   And be loyal to one's friends!'

And she,—she lies in my hand as tame
   As a pear late basking over a wall;
Just a touch to try and off it came;   35
   'Tis mine,—can I let it fall?

With no mind to eat it, that's the worst!
   Were it thrown in the road, would the case assist?
'Twas quenching a dozen blue-flies' thirst
   When I gave its stalk a twist.   40

And I,—what I seem to my friend, you see—
   What I soon shall seem to his love, you guess:
What I seem to myself, do you ask of me?
   No hero, I confess.

'Tis an awkward thing to play with souls,   45
   And matter enough to save one's own.
Yet think of my friend, and the burning coals
   He played with for bits of stone!

One likes to show the truth for the truth;
   That the woman was light is very true: 50
But suppose she says,—Never mind that youth—
   What wrong have I done to you?

Well, any how, here the story stays,
   So far at least I understand;
And, Robert Browning, you writer of plays,   55
   Here's a subject made to your hand!

Porphyria's Lover

The rain set early in to-night,
   The sullen wind was soon awake,
It tore the elm-tops down for spite,
   And did its worst to vex the lake:
   I listened with heart fit to break.   5
When glided in Porphyria; straight
   She shut the cold out and the storm,
And kneeled and made the cheerless grate
   Blaze up, and all the cottage warm;
   Which done, she rose, and from her form   10
Withdrew the dripping cloak and shawl,
   And laid her soiled gloves by, untied
Her hat and let the damp hair fall,
   And, last, she sat down by my side
   And called me. When no voice replied,   15
She put my arm about her waist,
   And made her smooth white shoulder bare,
And all her yellow hair displaced,
   And, stooping, made my cheek lie there,
   And spread, o'er all, her yellow hair,   20
Murmuring how she loved me—she
   Too weak, for all her heart's endeavour,
To set its struggling passion free
   From pride, and vainer ties dissever,
   And give herself to me for ever.   25

But passion sometimes would prevail,
   Nor could to-night's gay feast restrain
A sudden thought of one so pale
   For love of her, and all in vain:
     So, she was come through wind and rain.   30
Be sure I looked up at her eyes
   Happy and proud; at last I knew
Porphyria worshipped me; surprise
   Made my heart swell, and still it grew
     While I debated what to do.   35
That moment she was mine, mine, fair,
   Perfectly pure and good: I found
A thing to do, and all her hair
   In one long yellow string I wound
     Three times her little throat around,   40
And strangled her. No pain felt she;
   I am quite sure she felt no pain.
As a shut bud that holds a bee,
   I warily oped her lids: again
     Laughed the blue eyes without a stain.   45
And I untightened next the tress
   About her neck; her cheek once more
Blushed bright beneath my burning kiss:
   I propped her head up as before,
     Only, this time my shoulder bore   50
Her head, which droops upon it still:
   The smiling rosy little head,
So glad it has its utmost will,
   That all it scorned at once is fled,
     And I, its love, am gained instead!   55
Porphyria's love: she guessed not how
   Her darling one wish would be heard.
And thus we sit together now,
   And all night long we have not stirred,
     And yet God has not said a word!   60

My Last Duchess

Ferrara

That's my last Duchess painted on the wall,
Looking as if she were alive. I call
That piece a wonder, now: Frà Pandolf's hands
Worked busily a day, and there she stands.
Will't please you sit and look at her? I said   5
'Frà Pandolf' by design, for never read
Strangers like you that pictured countenance,
The depth and passion of its earnest glance,
But to myself they turned (since none puts by
The curtain I have drawn for you, but I)   10
And seemed as they would ask me, if they durst,
How such a glance came there; so, not the first
Are you to turn and ask thus. Sir, 't was not
Her husband's presence only, called that spot
Of joy into the Duchess' cheek: perhaps   15
Frà Pandolf chanced to say 'Her mantle laps
Over my lady's wrist too much,' or 'Paint
Must never hope to reproduce the faint
Half-flush that dies along her throat:' such stuff
Was courtesy, she thought, and cause enough   20
For calling up that spot of joy. She had
A heart—how shall I say?—too soon made glad,
Too easily impressed; she liked whate'er
She looked on, and her looks went everywhere.
Sir, 't was all one! My favour at her breast,   25
The dropping of the daylight in the West,
The bough of cherries some officious fool
Broke in the orchard for her, the white mule
She rode with round the terrace—all and each
Would draw from her alike the approving speech,   30
Or blush, at least. She thanked men,—good! but thanked
Somehow—I know not how—as if she ranked
My gift of a nine-hundred-years-old name
With anybody's gift. Who'd stoop to blame
This sort of trifling? Even had you skill   35
In speech—(which I have not)—to make your will

Quite clear to such an one, and say, 'Just this
Or that in you disgusts me; here you miss,
Or there exceed the mark'—and if she let
Herself be lessoned so, nor plainly set   40
Her wits to yours, forsooth, and made excuse,
—E'en then would be some stooping; and I choose
Never to stoop. Oh sir, she smiled, no doubt,
Whene'er I passed her; but who passed without
Much the same smile? This grew; I gave commands;   45
Then all smiles stopped together. There she stands
As if alive. Will't please you rise? We'll meet
The company below, then. I repeat,
The Count your master's known munificence
Is ample warrant that no just pretence   50
Of mine for dowry will be disallowed;
Though his fair daughter's self, as I avowed
At starting, is my object. Nay, we'll go
Together down, sir. Notice Neptune, though,
Taming a sea-horse, thought a rarity,   55
Which Claus of Innsbruck cast in bronze for me!

A Woman's Last Word

Let's contend no more, Love,
  Strive nor weep—
All be as before, Love,
  —Only sleep!

What so wild as words are?   5
  —I and thou
In debate, as birds are,
  Hawk on bough!

See the creature stalking
  While we speak—   10
Hush and hide the talking,
  Cheek on cheek!

What so false as truth is,
    False to thee?
Where the serpent's tooth is   15
    Shun the tree—

Where the apple reddens
    Never pry—
Lest we lose our Edens,
    Eve and I!   20

Be a god and hold me
    With a charm—
Be a man and fold me
    With thine arm!

Teach me, only teach, Love!   25
    As I ought
I will speak thy speech, Love,
    Think thy thought—

Meet, if thou require it,
    Both demands,   30
Laying flesh and spirit
    In thy hands!

That shall be to-morrow
    Not to-night:
I must bury sorrow   35
    Out of sight:

—Must a little weep, Love,
    Foolish me!—
And so fall asleep, Love,
    Loved by thee.   40

Two in the Campagna

I wonder do you feel to-day
    As I have felt since, hand in hand,
We sat down on the grass, to stray
    In spirit better through the land,
This morn of Rome and May?   5

For me, I touched a thought, I know,
    Has tantalized me many times,
(Like turns of thread the spiders throw
    Mocking across our path) for rhymes
To catch at and let go.   10

Help me to hold it! First it left
    The yellowing fennel, run to seed
There, branching from the brickwork's cleft,
    Some old tomb's ruin: yonder weed
Took up the floating weft,   15

Where one small orange cup amassed
    Five beetles,—blind and green they grope
Among the honey-meal: and last,
    Everywhere on the grassy slope
I traced it. Hold it fast!   20

The champaign with its endless fleece
    Of feathery grasses everywhere!
Silence and passion, joy and peace,
    And everlasting wash of air—
Rome's ghost since her decease.   25

Such life here, through such lengths of hours,
    Such miracles performed in play,
Such primal naked forms of flowers,
    Such letting nature have her way
While heaven looks from its towers!   30

How say you? Let us, O my dove,
   Let us be unashamed of soul,
As earth lies bare to heaven above!
   How is it under our control
To love or not to love?   35

I would that you were all to me,
   You that are just so much, no more.
Nor yours nor mine, nor slave nor free!
   Where does the fault lie? What the core
O' the wound, since wound must be?   40

I would I could adopt your will,
   See with your eyes, and set my heart
Beating by yours, and drink my fill
   At your soul's springs,—your part my part
In life, for good and ill.   45

No. I yearn upward, touch you close,
   Then stand away. I kiss your cheek,
Catch your soul's warmth,—I pluck the rose
   And love it more than tongue can speak—
Then the good minute goes.   50

Already how am I so far
   Out of that minute? Must I go
Still like the thistle-ball, no bar,
   Onward, whenever light winds blow.
Fixed by no friendly star?   55

Just when I seemed about to learn!
   Where is the thread now? Off again!
The old trick! Only I discern—
   Infinite passion, and the pain
Of finite hearts that yearn.   60

THOMAS HARDY
1840–1928

Thomas Hardy was born at Higher Bockhampton near Dorchester, and, apart from spells in London, he lived all his life in Dorset. As a young man he worked as an architect and it was on a visit to Cornwall to restore a church in 1874 that he met his first wife, Emma Gifford. In later years their marriage was not happy and Emma's death in 1912 drove Hardy to write some of his finest poems in an effort to preserve his memories of their first years together. In 1914 he married an old family friend, Florence Dugdale.

Hardy is most famous as a novelist and in prose and verse he explored the same basic themes, with a similar compassion and, at times, wry humour, repeatedly writing about nature's indifference to human suffering, failed love, and above all perhaps, time. Often, as in *The Going* and *At Castle Boterel* (two of the poems he wrote after Emma's death), he sets the past with all its potential against the sadness of the present. Too often human beings, like the tramp-woman in *The Trampwoman's Tragedy*, fail to see the consequences of their actions and spend their whole lives regretting a single mistake. He was acutely conscious, moreover, of human weakness and in poems like *In Church* often exposed the conceit which lies under an impressive exterior.

What makes reading Hardy's poetry a positive rather than depressing experience is what the later poet W. H. Auden calls Hardy's 'hawk's vision, his way of looking at life from a very great height', together with a capacity to present his beloved characters very closely, very intimately. Auden continues: 'To see the individual life related not only to the local social life of its time, but to the whole of human history . . . gives one both humility and self-confidence.' Humility because we as readers know that in time our experience might be similar to that which Hardy describes; self-confidence because we feel that we might, like Hardy, be able to face what happens and survive it.

Like Wordsworth, Hardy believed in using the language of everyday speech in his verse. He himself wrote in 1887 'that mere intellectual subtlety will not hold its own in time to come against the straightforward expression of true feeling.' But his own poems are not particularly 'straightforward'. They employ an extremely wide range of rhymes, and make use of subtle and varied metrical effects. As Philip Larkin puts it, almost every poem by Hardy 'has a little tune of its own. . . . Immediately you begin a Hardy poem your own inner response begins to rock in time with the poem's rhythm.' If you read the following poems aloud you will perhaps come to see what he means.

Snow in the Suburbs

       Every branch big with it,
       Bent every twig with it;
    Every fork like a white web-foot;
    Every street and pavement mute:
Some flakes have lost their way, and grope back upward, when   5
Meeting those meandering down they turn and descend again.
      The palings are glued together like a wall,
      And there is no waft of wind with the fleecy fall.

A sparrow enters the tree,
Whereon immediately   10
A snow-lump thrice his own slight size
Descends on him and showers his head and eyes,
And overturns him,
And near inurns him,
And lights on a nether twig, when its brush   15
Starts off a volley of other lodging lumps with a rush.

The steps are a blanched slope,
Up which, with feeble hope,
A black cat comes, wide-eyed and thin;
And we take him in.   20

In Church

'And now to God the Father,' he ends,
And his voice thrills up to the topmost tiles:
Each listener chokes as he bows and bends,
And emotion pervades the crowded aisles.
Then the preacher glides to the vestry-door,   5
And shuts it, and thinks he is seen no more.

The door swings softly ajar meanwhile,
And a pupil of his in the Bible class,
Who adores him as one without gloss or guile,
Sees her idol stand with a satisfied smile   10
And re-enact at the vestry-glass
Each pulpit gesture in deft dumb-show
That had moved the congregation so.

The Harbour Bridge

From here, the quay, one looks above to mark
The bridge across the harbour, hanging dark
Against the day's-end sky, fair-green in glow
Over and under the middle archway's bow:
It draws its skeleton where the sun has set,   5
Yea, clear from cutwater to parapet;
On which mild glow, too, lines of rope and spar
   Trace themselves black as char.

Down here in shade we hear the painters shift
Against the bollards with a drowsy lift,   10
As moved by the incoming stealthy tide.
High up across the bridge the burghers glide
As cut black-paper portraits hastening on
In conversation none knows what upon:
Their sharp-edged lips move quickly word by word   15
   To speech that is not heard.

There trails the dreamful girl, who leans and stops,
There presses the practical woman to the shops,
There is a sailor, meeting his wife with a start,
And we, drawn nearer, judge they are keeping apart.   20
Both pause. She says: 'I've looked for you. I thought
We'd make it up.' Then no words can be caught.
At last: 'Won't you come home?' She moves still nigher:
   ' 'Tis comfortable, with a fire.'

'No,' he says gloomily. 'And, anyhow,   25
I can't give up the other woman now:
You should have talked like that in former days,
When I was last home.' They go different ways.
And the west dims, and yellow lamplights shine:
And soon above, like lamps more opaline,   30
White stars ghost forth, that care not for men's wives,
   Or any other lives.

A Trampwoman's Tragedy

I

From Wynyard's Gap the livelong day,
    The livelong day,
We beat afoot the northward way
    We had travelled times before.
The sun-blaze burning on our backs,   5
Our shoulders sticking to our packs,
By fosseway, fields, and turnpike tracks
    We skirted sad Sedge-Moor.

II

Full twenty miles we jaunted on,
    We jaunted on, –   10
My fancy-man, and jeering John,
    And Mother Lee, and I.
And, as the sun drew down to west,
We climbed the toilsome Poldon crest,
And saw, of landskip sights the best,   15
    The inn that beamed thereby.

III

For months we had padded side by side,
    Ay, side by side
Through the Great Forest, Blackmoor wide,
    And where the Parret ran.   20
We'd faced the gusts on Mendip ridge,
Had crossed the Yeo unhelped by bridge,
Been stung by every Marshwood midge,
    I and my fancy-man.

IV

Lone inns we loved, my man and I,   25
    My man and I;
'King's Stag', 'Windwhistle' high and dry
    'The Horse' on Hintock Green,

The cosy house at Wynyard's Gap,
'The Hut' renowned on Bredy Knap,   30
And many another wayside tap
    Where folk might sit unseen.

     V
Now as we trudged – O deadly day,
    O deadly day! –
I teased my fancy-man in play   35
    And wanton idleness.
I walked alongside jeering John,
I laid his hand my waist upon;
I would not bend my glances on
    My lover's dark distress.   40

     VI
Thus Poldon top at last we won,
    At last we won,
And gained the inn at sink of sun
    Far-famed as 'Marshal's Elm'.
Beneath us figured tor and lea,   45
From Mendip to the western sea—
I doubt if finer sight there be
    Within this royal realm.

     VII
Inside the settle all a-row—
    All four a-row   50
We sat, I next to John, to show
    That he had wooed and won.
And then he took me on his knee,
And swore it was his turn to be
My favoured mate, and Mother Lee   55
    Passed to my former one.

     VIII
Then in a voice I had never heard,
    I had never heard,
My only Love to me: 'One word,
    My lady, if you please!   60

Whose is the child you are like to bear? –
His? After all my months o' care?'
God knows 'twas not! But, O despair!
      I nodded – still to tease.

IX

Then up he sprung, and with his knife—   65
      And with his knife
He let out jeering Johnny's life,
      Yes; there, at set of sun.
The slant ray through the window nigh
Gilded John's blood and glazing eye,   70
Ere scarcely Mother Lee and I
      Knew that the deed was done.

X

The taverns tell the gloomy tale,
      The gloomy tale,
How that at Ivel-chester jail   75
      My Love, my sweetheart swung;
Though stained till now by no misdeed
Save one horse ta'en in time o' need;
(Blue Jimmy stole right many a steed
      Ere his last fling he flung.)   80

XI

Thereaft I walked the world alone,
      Alone, alone!
On his death-day I gave my groan
      And dropt his dead-born child.
'Twas nigh the jail, beneath a tree,   85
None tending me; for Mother Lee
Had died at Glaston, leaving me
      Unfriended on the wild.

XII

And in the night as I lay weak,
      As I lay weak,   90
The leaves a-falling on my cheek,
      The red moon low declined—

The ghost of him I'd die to kiss
Rose up and said: 'Ah, tell me this!
Was the child mine, or was it his?   95
    Speak, that I rest may find!'

    XIII
O doubt not but I told him then,
    I told him then,
That I had kept me from all men
    Since we joined lips and swore.   100
Whereat he smiled, and thinned away
As the wind stirred to call up day . . .
—'Tis past! And here alone I stray
    Haunting the Western Moor.

Neutral Tones

We stood by a pond that winter day,
And the sun was white, as though chidden of God,
And a few leaves lay on the starving sod;
    —They had fallen from an ash, and were gray.

Your eyes on me were as eyes that rove   5
Over tedious riddles of years ago;
And some words played between us to and fro
    On which lost the more by our love.

The smile on your mouth was the deadest thing
Alive enough to have strength to die;   10
And a grin of bitterness swept thereby
    Like an ominous bird a-wing. . . .

Since then, keen lessons that love deceives,
And wrings with wrong, have shaped to me
Your face, and the God-curst sun, and a tree,   15
    And a pond edged with grayish leaves.

The Going

Why did you give no hint that night
That quickly after the morrow's dawn,
And calmly, as if indifferent quite,
You would close your term here, up and be gone
    Where I could not follow   5
    With wing of swallow
To gain one glimpse of you ever anon!

    Never to bid good-bye,
    Or lip me the softest call,
Or utter a wish for a word, while I   10
Saw morning harden upon the wall,
    Unmoved, unknowing
    That your great going
Had place that moment, and altered all.

Why do you make me leave the house   15
And think for a breath it is you I see
At the end of the alley of bending boughs
Where so often at dusk you used to be;
    Till in darkening dankness
    The yawning blankness   20
Of the perspective sickens me!

    You were she who abode
    By those red-veined rocks far West,
You were the swan-necked one who rode
Along the beetling Beeny Crest,   25
    And, reining nigh me,
    Would muse and eye me,
While Life unrolled us its very best.

Why, then, latterly did we not speak,
Did we not think of those days long dead,   30
And ere your vanishing strive to seek
That time's renewal? We might have said,
    'In this bright spring weather
    We'll visit together
Those places that once we visited.'   35

Well, well! All's past amend,
　　Unchangeable. It must go.
I seem but a dead man held on end
　To sink down soon. . . . O you could not know
　　　That such swift fleeing   40
　　　No soul foreseeing –
Not even I—would undo me so!

At Castle Boterel

As I drive to the junction of lane and highway,
　　And the drizzle bedrenches the waggonette,
I look behind at the fading byway,
　And see on its slope, now glistening wet,
　　　Distinctly yet   5

Myself and a girlish form benighted
　　In dry March weather. We climb the road
Beside a chaise. We had just alighted
　To ease the sturdy pony's load
　　　When he sighed and slowed.   10

What we did as we climbed, and what we talked of
　　Matters not much, nor to what it led,—
Something that life will not be balked of
　Without rude reason till hope is dead,
　　　And feeling fled.   15

It filled but a minute. But was there ever
　　A time of such quality, since or before,
In that hill's story? To one mind never,
　Though it has been climbed, foot-swift, foot-sore,
　　　By thousands more.   20

Primaeval rocks form the road's steep border,
   And much have they faced there, first and last,
Of the transitory in Earth's long order;
     But what they record in colour and cast
       Is—that we two passed.   25

And to me, though Time's unflinching rigour,
   In mindless rote, has ruled from sight
The substance now, one phantom figure
     Remains on the slope, as when that night
       Saw us alight.   30

I look and see it there, shrinking, shrinking,
   I look back at it amid the rain
For the very last time; for my sand is sinking,
     And I shall traverse old love's domain
       Never again.   35

The Darkling Thrush

I leant upon a coppice gate
    When Frost was spectre-gray,
And Winter's dregs made desolate
    The weakening eye of day.
The tangled bine-stems scored the sky   5
    Like strings of broken lyres,
And all mankind that haunted nigh
    Had sought their household fires.

The land's sharp features seemed to be
    The Century's corpse outleant,   10
His crypt the cloudy canopy,
    The wind his death-lament.
The ancient pulse of germ and birth
    Was shrunken hard and dry,
And every spirit upon earth   15
    Seemed fervourless as I.

At once a voice arose among
    The bleak twigs overhead
In a full-hearted evensong
    Of joy illimited;   20
An aged thrush, frail, gaunt, and small,
    In blast-beruffled plume,
Had chosen thus to fling his soul
    Upon the growing gloom.

So little cause for carolings   25
    Of such ecstatic sound
Was written on terrestrial things
    Afar or nigh around,
That I could think there trembled through
    His happy good-night air   30
Some blessed Hope, whereof he knew
    And I was unaware.

GERARD MANLEY HOPKINS
1844–1889

Hopkins spent most of his childhood in London and then studied Classics at Oxford where he became a Roman Catholic. In 1867 he decided to become a Jesuit priest, and a year later he took the vows of poverty, chastity and obedience which were to govern the rest of his life.

In his youth Hopkins had written rich, descriptive poetry in the manner of Keats. His religious convictions made him feel that poetry was a luxury which he should deny himself, and, on becoming a Jesuit, he stopped writing poetry for some years. In 1874, however, five nuns were drowned in the sinking of the ship the 'Deutschland', an event which led him to compose *The Wreck of the Deutschland*, a moving meditation on how God could allow such a tragedy.

From 1874 until the last years of his life Hopkins wrote the poems for which he is famous. These poems are for the most part intense celebrations of God's power as it is seen in nature. Hopkins was fascinated by the minute details of leaves, clouds, running water, stones and animals. He once even gave up looking at the sky for Lent, such was the pleasure he derived from it. As a priest, however, who was exposed to the harsh realities of life in the dark cities of industrial England, he was forced to sacrifice the outdoor pleasures he enjoyed and to face human poverty and physical ugliness. He came to feel that man had cheapened and failed to understand God's creation. In the poem *Binsey Poplars*, for instance, he expresses a sense of personal injury at the destruction of a line of trees in Oxford: for Hopkins each tree was sacred and irreplaceable.

Hopkins died of typhoid at the age of 45. His last years were unhappy ones. He had become Professor of Greek at University College, Dublin, where, over-burdened with the preparation of lectures and examination marking, he became physically weak and emotionally depressed by his sense that he was excluded from God's love. The so-called 'terrible sonnets' (*No worst, There is none* is included on page 81) are deeply expressive of his feelings of agony and despair at this time.

Since he never intended his poems for publication, few knew of their vividness and power until his friend Robert Bridges published a collection in 1918 which began to establish his reputation. Since then his highly individual style has led some readers to dismiss him as an eccentric and peculiar writer. Others have found this style perfectly suited to the expression both of his appreciation of nature and his spiritual experience.

God's Grandeur

The world is charged with the grandeur of God.
   It will flame out, like shining from shook foil;
   It gathers to a greatness, like the ooze of oil
Crushed. Why do men then now not reck his rod?
Generations have trod, have trod, have trod;   5
   And all is seared with trade; bleared, smeared with toil;
   And wears man's smudge and shares man's smell: the soil
Is bare now, nor can foot feel, being shod.

And for all this, nature is never spent;
   There lives the dearest freshness deep down things;   10
And though the last lights off the black West went
   Oh, morning, at the brown brink eastward, springs –
Because the Holy Ghost over the bent
   World broods with warm breast and with ah! bright wings.

Spring

Nothing is so beautiful as spring—
   When weeds, in wheels, shoot long and lovely and lush;
   Thrush's eggs look little low heavens, and thrush
Through the echoing timber does so rinse and wring
The ear, it strikes like lightnings to hear him sing;   5
   The glassy peartree leaves and blooms, they brush
   The descending blue; that blue is all in a rush
With richness; the racing lambs too have fair their fling.

What is all this juice and all this joy?
   A strain of the earth's sweet being in the beginning   10
In Eden garden.—Have, get, before it cloy,
   Before it cloud, Christ, lord, and sour with sinning,
Innocent mind and Mayday in girl and boy,
   Most, O maid's child, thy choice and worthy the winning.

Hurrahing in Harvest

Summer ends now; now, barbarous in beauty, the stooks rise
   Around; up above, what wind-walks! what lovely behaviour
   Of silk-sack clouds! has wilder, wilful-wavier
Meal-drift moulded ever and melted across skies?

I walk, I lift up, I lift up heart, eyes,   5
   Down all that glory in the heavens to glean our Saviour;
   And, éyes, heárt, what looks, what lips yet gave you a
Rapturous love's greeting of realer, of rounder replies?

And the azurous hung hills are his world-wielding shoulder
    Majestic—as a stallion stalwart, very-violet-sweet!—   10
These things, these things were here and but the beholder
    Wanting; which two when they once meet,
The heart rears wings bold and bolder
    And hurls for him, O half hurls earth for him off under his
feet.

Binsey Poplars

felled 1879

My aspens dear, whose airy cages quelled,
  Quelled or quenched in leaves the leaping sun,
All felled, felled, are all felled;
    Of a fresh and following folded rank
            Not spared, not one   5
          That dandled a sandalled
      Shadow that swam or sank
On meadow and river and wind-wandering
  weed-winding bank.

    O if we but knew what we do
        When we delve or hew –   10
      Hack and rack the growing green!
        Since country is so tender
    To touch, her being só slender,
    That, like this sleek and seeing ball
    But a prick will make no eye at all,   15
    Where we, even where we mean
        To mend her we end her,
      When we hew or delve:
After-comers cannot guess the beauty been.
    Ten or twelve, only ten or twelve   20
      Strokes of havoc únselve
        The sweet especial scene,
    Rural scene, a rural scene,
    Sweet especial rural scene.

Felix Randal

Felix Randal the farrier, O is he dead then? my duty all ended,
Who have watched his mould of man, big-boned and
    hardy-handsome
Pining, pining, till time when reason rambled in it and some
Fatal four disorders, fleshed there, all contended?

Sickness broke him. Impatient he cursed at first, but mended   5
Being anointed and all; though a heavenlier heart began some
Months earlier, since I had our sweet reprieve and ransom
Tendered to him. Ah well, God rest him all road ever he
    offended!

This seeing the sick endears them to us, us too it endears.
My tongue had taught thee comfort, touch had quenched thy
    tears,   10
Thy tears that touched my heart, child, Felix, poor Felix Randal;

How far from then forethought of, all thy more boisterous years,
When thou at the random grim forge, powerful amidst peers,
Didst fettle for the great grey drayhorse his bright and battering
    sandal!

No worst, there is none

No worst, there is none. Pitched past pitch of grief,
More pangs will, schooled at forepangs, wilder wring.
Comforter, where, where is your comforting?
Mary, mother of us, where is your relief?
My cries heave, herds-long; huddle in a main, a chief-   5
woe, world-sorrow; on an age-old anvil wince and sing—
Then lull, then leave off. Fury had shrieked 'No ling-
ering! Let me be fell: force I must be brief.'

    O the mind, mind has mountains; cliffs of fall
Frightful, sheer, no-man-fathomed. Hold them cheap   10
May who ne'er hung there. Nor does long our small
Durance deal with that steep or deep. Here! creep,
Wretch, under a comfort serves in a whirlwind: all
Life death does end and each day dies with sleep.

W. B. YEATS
1865–1939

William Butler Yeats was born in Dublin and educated in Ireland and England. He was a lonely and often unhappy boy who spent much of his time day-dreaming and writing escapist poetry. 'I was humiliated,' he confessed later, 'and wrote always of proud, confident men and women.' On leaving school, he studied art for a while in Dublin. He soon abandoned painting, but two interests which he developed at this time stayed with him for the rest of his life: his enthusiasm for magic and psychical research and his involvement in the Irish nationalist movement. In 1889 he met Maud Gonne, a leading figure in the struggle to throw off British rule and the woman who was to dominate his life for the next twenty years. The unhappiness Yeats felt at Maud Gonne's refusal to marry him underlies many of his poems.

During the first years of the twentieth century, much of Yeats's energy went into running the Abbey Theatre in Dublin, but he continued to write poems and in 1923 was awarded the Nobel prize for literature. At the age of 52, Yeats married Georgina Hyde-Lees, and during the 1920s he became a member of the Irish Senate. His health gradually deteriorated and he died in France in 1939. After the war his body was brought back to Ireland and buried in Drumcliffe churchyard, near to the town of Sligo he had known as a boy. On his grave are written these words from one of his last poems:

> Cast a cold eye
> On life, on death.
> Horseman, pass by!

Yeats made his poems from his sense of Ireland and its history, from his interest in magic, and from his often frustrating relationships with women. He once described his early poems as being 'blurred with desire and vague regret', and his style certainly grew more vigorous as he came in middle-age to explore his feelings more directly and analytically.

In his later collections of poems (particularly *The Tower* and *The Winding Stair*) this style develops remarkably, as he attempts to relate his own life, as man and artist, to time and eternity. It is Yeats's refusal ever to rest content with an easy solution to the problems which he faced which is ultimately the most impressive thing about his poetry. 'Myself must I remake', he wrote in a late poem, and this is precisely what he tried, throughout his life and through his poetry, to do.

The Song of Wandering Aengus

I went out to the hazel wood,
Because a fire was in my head,
And cut and peeled a hazel wand,
And hooked a berry to a thread;
And when white moths were on the wing,   5
And moth-like stars were flickering out,
I dropped the berry in a stream
And caught a little silver trout.

When I had laid it on the floor
I went to blow the fire aflame,   10
But something rustled on the floor,
And some one called me by my name:
It had become a glimmering girl
With apple blossom in her hair
Who called me by my name and ran   15
And faded through the brightening air.

Though I am old with wandering
Through hollow lands and hilly lands,
I will find out where she has gone,
And kiss her lips and take her hands;   20
And walk among long dappled grass,
And pluck till time and times are done
The silver apples of the moon,
The golden apples of the sun.

He Wishes for
the Cloths of Heaven

Had I the heavens' embroidered cloths,
Enwrought with golden and silver light,
The blue and the dim and the dark cloths
Of night and light and the half-light,
I would spread the cloths under your feet: 5
But I, being poor, have only my dreams;
I have spread my dreams under your feet;
Tread softly because you tread on my dreams.

Adam's Curse

We sat together at one summer's end,
That beautiful mild woman, your close friend,
And you and I, and talked of poetry.
I said, 'A line will take us hours maybe;
Yet if it does not seem a moment's thought,   5
Our stitching and unstitching has been naught.

Better go down upon your marrow-bones
And scrub a kitchen pavement, or break stones
Like an old pauper, in all kinds of weather;
For to articulate sweet sounds together   10
Is to work harder than all these, and yet
Be thought an idler by the noisy set
Of bankers, schoolmasters, and clergymen
The martyrs call the world.'

               And thereupon   15
That beautiful mild woman for whose sake
There's many a one shall find out all heartache
On finding that her voice is sweet and low
Replied, 'To be born woman is to know—
Although they do not talk of it at school—   20
That we must labour to be beautiful.'

I said, 'It's certain there is no fine thing
Since Adam's fall but needs much labouring.
There have been lovers who thought love should be
So much compounded of high courtesy   25
That they would sigh and quote with learned looks
Precedents out of beautiful old books;
Yet now it seems an idle trade enough.'

We sat grown quiet at the name of love;
We saw the last embers of daylight die,   30
And in the trembling blue-green of the sky
A moon, worn as if it had been a shell
Washed by time's waters as they rose and fell
About the stars and broke in days and years.

I had a thought for no one's but your ears: 35
That you were beautiful, and that I strove
To love you in the old high way of love;
That it had all seemed happy, and yet we'd grown
As weary-hearted as that hollow moon.

The Wild Swans at Coole

The trees are in their autumn beauty,
The woodland paths are dry,
Under the October twilight the water
Mirrors a still sky;
Upon the brimming water among the stones   5
Are nine-and-fifty swans.

The nineteenth autumn has come upon me
Since I first made my count;
I saw, before I had well finished,
All suddenly mount   10
And scatter wheeling in great broken rings
Upon their clamorous wings.

I have looked upon those brilliant creatures,
And now my heart is sore.
All's changed since I, hearing at twilight,   15
The first time on this shore,
The bell-beat of their wings above my head,
Trod with a lighter tread.

Unwearied still, lover by lover,
They paddle in the cold   20
Companionable streams or climb the air;
Their hearts have not grown old;
Passion or conquest, wander where they will,
Attend upon them still.

But now they drift on the still water,   25
Mysterious, beautiful;
Among what rushes will they build,
By what lake's edge or pool
Delight men's eyes when I awake some day
To find they have flown away?   30

Broken Dreams

There is grey in your hair.
Young men no longer suddenly catch their breath
When you are passing;
But maybe some old gaffer mutters a blessing
Because it was your prayer   5
Recovered him upon the bed of death.
For your sole sake—that all heart's ache have known,
And given to others all heart's ache,
From meagre girlhood's putting on
Burdensome beauty—for your sole sake   10
Heaven has put away the stroke of her doom,
So great her portion in that peace you make
By merely walking in a room.

Your beauty can but leave among us
Vague memories, nothing but memories.   15
A young man when the old men are done talking
Will say to an old man, 'Tell me of that lady
The poet stubborn with his passion sang us
When age might well have chilled his blood.'

Vague memories, nothing but memories,   20
But in the grave all, all, shall be renewed.
The certainty that I shall see that lady
Leaning or standing or walking
In the first loveliness of womanhood,
And with the fervour of my youthful eyes,   25
Has set me muttering like a fool.

You are more beautiful than any one,
And yet your body had a flaw:
Your small hands were not beautiful,
And I am afraid that you will run   30
And paddle to the wrist
In that mysterious, always brimming lake
Where those that have obeyed the holy law
Paddle and are perfect. Leave unchanged
The hands that I have kissed,   35
For old sake's sake.

The last stroke of midnight dies.
All day in the one chair
From dream to dream and rhyme to rhyme I have ranged
In rambling talk with an image of air: 40
Vague memories, nothing but memories.

The Second Coming

Turning and turning in the widening gyre
The falcon cannot hear the falconer;
Things fall apart; the centre cannot hold;
Mere anarchy is loosed upon the world,
The blood-dimmed tide is loosed, and everywhere   5
The ceremony of innocence is drowned;
The best lack all conviction, while the worst
Are full of passionate intensity.

Surely some revelation is at hand;
Surely the Second Coming is at hand.   10
The Second Coming! Hardly are those words out
When a vast image out of *Spiritus Mundi*
Troubles my sight: somewhere in sands of the desert
A shape with lion body and the head of a man,
A gaze blank and pitiless as the sun,   15
Is moving its slow thighs, while all about it
Reel shadows of the indignant desert birds.
The darkness drops again; but now I know
That twenty centuries of stony sleep
Were vexed to nightmare by a rocking cradle,   20
And what rough beast, its hour come round at last,
Slouches towards Bethlehem to be born?

A Prayer for My Daughter

Once more the storm is howling, and half hid
Under this cradle-hood and coverlid
My child sleeps on. There is no obstacle
But Gregory's wood and one bare hill
Whereby the haystack- and roof-levelling wind,   5
Bred on the Atlantic, can be stayed;
And for an hour I have walked and prayed
Because of the great gloom that is in my mind.

I have walked and prayed for this young child an hour
And heard the sea-wind scream upon the tower,   10
And under the arches of the bridge, and scream
In the elms above the flooded stream;
Imagining in excited reverie
That the future years had come,
Dancing to a frenzied drum,   15
Out of the murderous innocence of the sea.

May she be granted beauty and yet not
Beauty to make a stranger's eye distraught,
Or hers before a looking-glass, for such,
Being made beautiful overmuch,   20
Consider beauty a sufficient end,
Lose natural kindness and maybe
The heart-revealing intimacy
That chooses right, and never find a friend.

Helen being chosen found life flat and dull   25
And later had much trouble from a fool,
While that great Queen, that rose out of the spray,
Being fatherless could have her way
Yet chose a bandy-leggèd smith for man.
It's certain that fine women eat   30
A crazy salad with their meat
Whereby the Horn of Plenty is undone.

In courtesy I'd have her chiefly learned;
Hearts are not had as a gift but hearts are earned

By those that are not entirely beautiful;   35
Yet many, that have played the fool
For beauty's very self, has charm made wise,
And many a poor man that has roved,
Loved and thought himself beloved,
From a glad kindness cannot take his eyes.   40

May she become a flourishing hidden tree
That all her thoughts may like the linnet be,
And have no business but dispensing round
Their magnanimities of sound,
Nor but in merriment begin a chase,   45
Nor but in merriment a quarrel.
O may she live like some green laurel
Rooted in one dear perpetual place.

My mind, because the minds that I have loved,
The sort of beauty that I have approved,   50
Prosper but little, has dried up of late,
Yet knows that to be choked with hate
May well be of all evil chances chief.
If there's no hatred in a mind
Assault and battery of the wind   55
Can never tear the linnet from the leaf.

An intellectual hatred is the worst,
So let her think opinions are accursed.
Have I not seen the loveliest woman born
Out of the mouth of Plenty's horn,   60
Because of her opinionated mind
Barter that horn and every good
By quiet natures understood
For an old bellows full of angry wind?

Considering that, all hatred driven hence,   65
The soul recovers radical innocence
And learns at last that it is self-delighting,
Self-appeasing, self-affrighting,
And that its own sweet will is Heaven's will;

She can, though every face should scowl   70
And every windy quarter howl
Or every bellows burst, be happy still.

And may her bridegroom bring her to a house
Where all's accustomed, ceremonious;
For arrogance and hatred are the wares   75
Peddled in the thoroughfares.
How but in custom and in ceremony
Are innocence and beauty born?
Ceremony's a name for the rich horn,
And custom for the spreading laurel tree.   80

EDWARD THOMAS
1878–1917

Edward Thomas was born in London but spent most of his adult life in Hampshire. While still a student at Oxford he married Helen Noble and supported her and their three children, through his writing, until he enlisted in the Artists' Rifles in 1915. Financial pressures meant that during these years he had to compile anthologies, prepare hundreds of book reviews, and write over thirty books on literary and topographical subjects. This unceasing work could not have helped the serious bouts of depression from which he frequently suffered. It was not until 1912 when he met the American poet, Robert Frost, that Thomas found the confidence to write poetry, and it was only in the last two years of his life after he had enlisted as a soldier that he had the financial security to concentrate upon the writing of poetry. He was killed by a shell at the battle of Arras on Easter Monday, 9 April 1917.

Thomas's reputation as a poet grew slowly. For many years he was read, if he was read at all, for his finely detailed descriptions of the English countryside. Few readers recognized that his poetry was as much about himself as it was about nature. In *March*, for instance, the springtime weather and its effect on the thrushes' song are observed with delicate and evocative precision. But after reading the poem we are left with a sense of the man who experienced 'the cold burning/Of hail and wind', who was fighting his own wintry depressions, and who hoped that sometime, 'perhaps tomorrow', a new spring might return to his own life. These personal preoccupations emerge with remarkable delicacy from the physical description. It was Thomas's greatest gift as a poet that he could let the natural world be itself so that it could speak all the more movingly for him.

In a letter to his friend, Eleanor Farjeon, Thomas wrote that he was trying in his poetry 'to get rid of the last rags of rhetoric and formality which often left my prose with a dead rhythm'. He often succeeded. The unassuming, colloquial vocabulary and natural rhythms of his best poems reflect the movement of everyday speech. More often than not, he allows the experience he is writing about to determine the line-length, the use or non-use of rhyme, the overall length of the poem. There is, however, nothing casual about his craftsmanship, and a close reading of any of the poems printed in this selection will show how carefully and sensitively Thomas chose and ordered his words.

The Signpost

The dim sea glints chill. The white sun is shy,
And the skeleton weeds and the never-dry,
Rough, long grasses keep white with frost
At the hilltop by the finger-post;
The smoke of traveller's-joy is puffed   5
Over hawthorn berry and hazel tuft.

I read the sign. Which way shall I go?
A voice says: You would not have doubted so
At twenty. Another voice gentle with scorn
Says: At twenty you wished you had never been born.   10

One hazel lost a leaf of gold
From a tuft at the tip, when the first voice told
The other he wished to know what 'twould be
To be sixty by this same post. 'You shall see'
He laughed—and I had to join his laughter—   15
'You shall see; but either before or after,
Whatever happens, it must befall,
A mouthful of earth to remedy all
Regrets and wishes shall freely be given;
And if there be a flaw in that heaven   20
'Twill be freedom to wish, and your wish may be
To be here or anywhere talking to me,
No matter what the weather, on earth,
At any age between death and birth,
To see what day or night can be,   25
The sun and the frost, the land and the sea,
Summer, Autumn, Winter, Spring,
With a poor man of any sort, down to a king,
Standing upright out in the air
Wondering where he shall journey, O where?'   30

March

Now I know that Spring will come again,
Perhaps tomorrow: however late I've patience
After this night following on such a day.

While still my temples ached from the cold burning
Of hail and wind, and still the primroses   5
Torn by the hail were covered up in it,
The sun filled earth and heaven with a great light
And a tenderness, almost warmth, where the hail dripped,
As if the mighty sun wept tears of joy.
But 'twas too late for warmth. The sunset piled   10
Mountains on mountains of snow and ice in the west:
Somewhere among their folds the wind was lost,
And yet 'twas cold, and though I knew that Spring
Would come again, I knew it had not come,
That it was lost too in those mountains chill.   15

What did the thrushes know? Rain, snow, sleet, hail,
Had kept them quiet as the primroses.
They had but an hour to sing. On boughs they sang,
On gates, on ground; they sang while they changed perches
And while they fought, if they remembered to fight: 20
So earnest were they to pack into that hour
Their unwilling hoard of song before the moon
Grew brighter than the clouds. Then 'twas no time
For singing merely. So they could keep off silence
And night, they cared not what they sang or screamed;   25
Whether 'twas hoarse or sweet or fierce or soft;
And to me all was sweet: they could do no wrong.
Something they knew—I also, while they sang
And after. Not till night had half its stars
And never a cloud, was I aware of silence   30
Stained with all that hour's songs, a silence
Saying that Spring returns, perhaps tomorrow.

After Rain

The rain of a night and a day and a night
Stops at the light
Of this pale choked day. The peering sun
Sees what has been done.
The road under the trees has a border new   5
Of purple hue
Inside the border of bright thin grass:
For all that has
Been left by November of leaves is torn
From hazel and thorn   10
And the greater trees. Throughout the copse
No dead leaf drops
On grey grass, green moss, burnt-orange fern,
At the wind's return:
The leaflets out of the ash-tree shed   15
Are thinly spread
In the road, like little black fish, inlaid,
As if they played.

What hangs from the myriad branches down there
So hard and bare   20
Is twelve yellow apples lovely to see
On one crab-tree,
And on each twig of every tree in the dell
Uncountable
Crystals both dark and bright of the rain   25
That begins again.

Beauty

What does it mean? Tired, angry, and ill at ease,
No man, woman, or child, alive could please
Me now. And yet I almost dare to laugh
Because I sit and frame an epitaph—
'Here lies all that no one loved of him   5
And that loved no one.' Then in a trice that whim
Has wearied. But, though I am like a river
At fall of evening while it seems that never
Has the sun lighted it or warmed it, while
Cross breezes cut the surface to a file,   10
This heart, some fraction of me, happily
Floats through the window even now to a tree
Down in the misting, dim-lit, quiet vale,
Not like a pewit that returns to wail
For something it has lost, but like a dove   15
That slants unswerving to its home and love.
There I find my rest, as through the dusk air
Flies what yet lives in me: Beauty is there.

The Path

Running along a bank, a parapet
That saves from the precipitous wood below
The level road, there is a path. It serves
Children for looking down the long smooth steep,
Between the legs of beech and yew, to where   5
A fallen tree checks the sight: while men and women

Content themselves with the road and what they see
Over the bank, and what the children tell.
The path, winding like silver, trickles on,
Bordered and even invaded by thinnest moss   10
That tries to cover roots and crumbling chalk
With gold, olive, and emerald, but in vain.
The children wear it. They have flattened the bank
On top, and silvered it between the moss
With the current of their feet, year after year.   15
But the road is houseless, and leads not to school.
To see a child is rare there, and the eye
Has but the road, the wood that overhangs
And underyawns it, and the path that looks
As if it led on to some legendary   20
Or fancied place where men have wished to go
And stay; till, sudden, it ends where the wood ends.

October

The green elm with the one great bough of gold
Lets leaves into the grass slip, one by one.—
The short hill grass, the mushrooms small milk-white,
Harebell and scabious and tormentil,
That blackberry and gorse, in dew and sun,   5
Bow down to; and the wind travels too light
To shake the fallen birch leaves from the fern;
The gossamers wander at their own will.
At heavier steps than birds' the squirrels scold.

The late year has grown fresh again and new   10
As Spring, and to the touch is not more cool
Than it is warm to the gaze; and now I might
As happy be as earth is beautiful,
Were I some other or with earth could turn
In alternation of violet and rose,   15
Harebell and snowdrop, at their season due,
And gorse that has no time not to be gay.
But if this be not happiness, who knows?
Some day I shall think this a happy day,
And this mood by the name of melancholy   20
Shall no more blackened and obscured be.

As the team's head brass

As the team's head brass flashed out on the turn
The lovers disappeared into the wood.
I sat among the boughs of the fallen elm
That strewed an angle of the fallow, and
Watched the plough narrowing a yellow square   5
Of charlock. Every time the horses turned
Instead of treading me down, the ploughman leaned
Upon the handles to say or ask a word,
About the weather, next about the war.
Scraping the share he faced towards the wood,   10
And screwed along the furrow till the brass flashed
Once more.
        The blizzard felled the elm whose crest
I sat in, by a woodpecker's round hole,
The ploughman said, 'When will they take it away?'
'When the war's over.' So the talk began—   15
One minute and an interval of ten,
A minute more and the same interval.
'Have you been out?' 'No.' 'And don't want to, perhaps?'
'If I could only come back again, I should.
I could spare an arm. I shouldn't want to lose   20
A leg. If I should lose my head, why, so,
I should want nothing more. . . . Have many gone
From here?' 'Yes.' 'Many lost?' 'Yes, a good few.
Only two teams work on the farm this year.
One of my mates is dead. The second day   25
In France they killed him. It was back in March,
The very night of the blizzard, too. Now if
He had stayed here we should have moved the tree.'
'And I should not have sat here. Everything
Would have been different. For it would have been   30
Another world.' 'Ay, and a better, though
If we could see all all might seem good.' Then
The lovers came out of the wood again:
The horses started and for the last time
I watched the clods crumble and topple over   35
After the ploughshare and the stumbling team.

D. H. LAWRENCE
1885–1930

David Herbert Lawrence was born in Eastwood in Nottingham-shire. His father was a coalminer, and Lawrence's early novel, *Sons and Lovers*, gives a vivid picture of what life was then like in a mining community. A bright boy encouraged by an ambitious mother, he was educated at Nottingham High School and University College, Nottingham, where he qualified as a teacher. He taught for only three years, and in 1912, after a serious illness and having published his first novel, *The White Peacock*, devoted himself to his writing. In the same year he eloped to Germany with Frieda Weekley, the wife of his former Professor at Nottingham. They married in 1914, and, after spending most of the First World War in Cornwall, travelled through Europe, to Ceylon, Australia, and to New Mexico. They returned to Italy in 1925, and Lawrence died of tuberculosis in the south of France on 2 March 1930 at the age of 44.

Many of Lawrence's poems make no use of rhymes or pre-conceived metrical patterns. They are written in what is known as 'free verse', and some readers have argued that this lack of formal structure is evidence of Lawrence's carelessness as a poet. Lawrence, in fact, abandoned traditional poetic form quite deliberately. He wanted in his poetry to express his emotions in their immediacy and complexity, and felt that free verse was the best way in which he could do this. 'Free verse,' he once wrote, 'has its own *nature*. . . . It has no finish. It has no satisfying stability, satisfying for those who like the immutable. None of this. It is the instant; the quick.' His best poems certainly give powerful and moving expression to his feelings, the shape of each poem being determined by the nature of the feeling Lawrence is attempting to express. Whether this approach to poetry amounts to 'carelessness' is something you could consider.

What no selection of Lawrence's poetry can begin to communicate is the sheer range of emotion which can be found if you read through the *Collected Poems* as a whole. Lawrence once said that many of his poems were 'so personal that, in their fragmentary fashion, they make up a biography of an emotional and inner life'. This selection offers glimpses of his 'emotional and inner life', and, it is hoped, a sense of Lawrence's determination never to play with his feelings in a self-indulgent fashion. He wanted to understand what he felt, to gain control over his emotions so that he could grow not just as a poet but as a man. Which is why he wrote in a letter he sent to a friend in 1917: 'Art itself doesn't interest me, only the spiritual content'. How much this is an exaggeration is something else to consider.

Discord in Childhood

Outside the house an ash-tree hung its terrible whips,
And at night when the wind rose, the lash of the tree
Shrieked and slashed the wind, as a ship's
Weird rigging in a storm shrieks hideously.

Within the house two voices arose, a slender lash   5
Whistling she-delirious rage, and the dreadful sound
Of a male thong booming and bruising, until it had drowned
The other voice in a silence of blood, 'neath the noise of the ash.

Piano

Softly, in the dusk, a woman is singing to me;
Taking me back down the vista of years, till I see
A child sitting under the piano, in the boom of the tingling
    strings
And pressing the small, poised feet of a mother who smiles as
    she sings.

In spite of myself, the insidious mastery of song   5
Betrays me back, till the heart of me weeps to belong
To the old Sunday evenings at home, with winter outside
And hymns in the cosy parlour, the tinkling piano our guide.

So now it is vain for the singer to burst into clamour
With the great black piano appassionato. The glamour   10
Of childish days is upon me, my manhood is cast
Down in the flood of remembrance, I weep like a child for
    the past.

The Best of School

The blinds are drawn because of the sun,
And the boys and the room in a colourless gloom
Of underwater float: bright ripples run
Across the walls as the blinds are blown
To let the sunlight in; and I,   5
As I sit on the shores of the class, alone,
Watch the boys in their summer blouses
As they write, their round heads busily bowed:
And one after another rouses
His face to look at me,   10
To ponder very quietly,
As seeing, he does not see.

And then he turns again, with a little glad
Thrill of his work he turns again from me,   15
Having found what he wanted, having got what was
    to be had.

And very sweet it is, while the sunlight waves
In the ripening morning, to sit alone with the class
And feel the stream of awakening ripple and pass
From me to the boys, whose brightening souls it laves   20
For this little hour.

       This morning, sweet it is
To feel the lads' looks light on me,
Then back in a swift, bright flutter to work;
Each one darting away with his
Discovery, like birds that steal and flee.   25

Touch after touch I feel on me
As their eyes glance at me for the grain
Of rigour they taste delightedly.

As tendrils reach out yearningly,
Slowly rotate till they touch the tree   30
That they cleave unto, and up which they climb
Up to their lives—so they to me.

I feel them cling and cleave to me
As vines going eagerly up; they twine
My life with other leaves, my time   35
Is hidden in theirs, their thrills are mine.

Last Lesson of the Afternoon

When will the bell ring, and end this weariness?
How long have they tugged the leash, and strained apart,
My pack of unruly hounds! I cannot start
Them again on a quarry of knowledge they hate to hunt,
I can haul them and urge them no more.   5

No longer now can I endure the brunt
Of the books that lie out on the desks; a full threescore
Of several insults of blotted pages, and scrawl
Of slovenly work that they have offered me.
I am sick, and what on earth is the good of it all?   10
What good to them or me, I cannot see!

So, shall I take
My last dear fuel of life to heap on my soul
And kindle my will to a flame that shall consume
Their dross of indifference; and take the toll   15
Of their insults in punishment?—I will not!—

I will not waste my soul and my strength for this.
What do I care for all that they do amiss!
What is the point of this teaching of mine, and of this
Learning of theirs? It all goes down the same abyss.   20

What does it matter to me, if they can write
A description of a dog, or if they can't?
What is the point? To us both, it is all my aunt!
And yet I'm supposed to care, with all my might.

I do not, and will not; they won't and they don't; and that's all!   25
I shall keep my strength for myself; they can keep theirs as well.
Why should we beat our heads against the wall
Of each other? I shall sit and wait for the bell.

Snake

A snake came to my water-trough
On a hot, hot day, and I in pyjamas for the heat,
To drink there.

In the deep, strange-scented shade of the great dark carob-tree
I came down the steps with my pitcher   5
And must wait, must stand and wait, for there he was at the
    trough before me.

He reached down from a fissure in the earth-wall in the gloom
And trailed his yellow-brown slackness soft-bellied down, over
    the edge of the stone trough
And rested his throat upon the stone bottom,

And where the water had dripped from the tap, in a small
  clearness,   10
He sipped with his straight mouth,
Softly drank through his straight gums, into his slack long body,
Silently.

Someone was before me at my water-trough,
And I, like a second comer, waiting.   15

He lifted his head from his drinking, as cattle do,
And looked at me vaguely, as drinking cattle do,
And flickered his two-forked tongue from his lips, and
  mused a moment,
And stooped and drank a little more,
Being earth-brown, earth-golden from the burning bowels
  of the earth   20
On the day of Sicilian July, with Etna smoking.

The voice of my education said to me
He must be killed,
For in Sicily the black, black snakes are innocent, the gold
  are venomous.

And voices in me said, If you were a man   25
You would take a stick and break him now, and finish
  him off.

But must I confess how I liked him,
How glad I was he had come like a guest in quiet, to drink
  at my water-trough
And depart peaceful, pacified, and thankless,
Into the burning bowels of this earth?   30

Was it cowardice, that I dared not kill him?
Was it perversity, that I longed to talk to him?
Was it humility, to feel so honoured?
I felt so honoured.

And yet those voices: 35
If you were not afraid, you would kill him!
And truly I was afraid, I was most afraid,

But even so, honoured still more
That he should seek my hospitality
From out the dark door of the secret earth.   40

He drank enough
And lifted his head, dreamily, as one who has drunken,
And flickered his tongue like a forked night on the air, so
    black,
Seeming to lick his lips,
And looked around like a god, unseeing, into the air,   45
And slowly turned his head,
And slowly, very slowly, as if thrice adream,
Proceeded to draw his slow length curving round
And climb again the broken bank of my wall-face.

And as he put his head into that dreadful hole,   50
And as he slowly drew up, snake-easing his shoulders, and
    entered farther,
A sort of horror, a sort of protest against his withdrawing
    into that horrid black hole,
Deliberately going into the blackness, and slowly drawing
    himself after,
Overcame me now his back was turned.

I looked round, I put down my pitcher,   55
I picked up a clumsy log
And threw it at the water-trough with a clatter.

I think it did not hit him,
But suddenly that part of him that was left behind convulsed
    in undignified haste,
Writhed like lightning, and was gone   60
Into the black hole, the earth-lipped fissure in the wall-front,
At which, in the intense still noon, I stared with fascination.

And immediately I regretted it.
I thought how paltry, how vulgar, what a mean act!
I despised myself and the voices of my accursed human
    education.   65

And I thought of the albatross,
And I wished he would come back, my snake.

For he seemed to me again like a king,
Like a king in exile, uncrowned in the underworld,
Now due to be crowned again.   70

And so, I missed my chance with one of the lords
Of life.
And I have something to expiate;
A pettiness.

Bavarian Gentians

Not every man has gentians in his house
in soft September, at slow, sad Michaelmas.

Bavarian gentians, big and dark, only dark
darkening the day-time, torch-like with the smoking blueness of
    Pluto's gloom,
ribbed and torch-like, with their blaze of darkness spread blue   5
down flattening into points, flattened under the sweep of white
    day
torch-flower of the blue-smoking darkness, Pluto's dark-blue
    daze,
black lamps from the halls of Dis, burning dark blue,
giving off darkness, blue darkness, as Demeter's pale lamps
    give off light,
lead me then, lead the way.   10

Reach me a gentian, give me a torch!
let me guide myself with the blue, forked torch of this flower
down the darker and darker stairs, where blue is darkened on
    blueness
even where Persephone goes, just now, from the frosted
    September
to the sightless realm where darkness is awake upon the dark   15
and Persephone herself is but a voice
or a darkness invisible enfolded in the deeper dark
of the arms Plutonic, and pierced with the passion of dense
    gloom,
among the splendour of torches of darkness, shedding darkness
    on the lost bride and her groom.

The Ship of Death

I

Now it is autumn and the falling fruit
and the long journey towards oblivion.

The apples falling like great drops of dew
to bruise themselves an exit from themselves.

And it is time to go, to bid farewell   5
to one's own self, and find an exit
from the fallen self.

II

Have you built your ship of death, O have you?
O build your ship of death, for you will need it.
The grim frost is at hand, when the apples will fall   10
thick, almost thundrous, on the hardened earth.

And death is on the air like a smell of ashes!
Ah! can't you smell it?

And in the bruised body, the frightened soul
finds itself shrinking, wincing from the cold   15
that blows upon it through the orifices.

III

And can a man his own quietus make
with a bare bodkin?

With daggers, bodkins, bullets, man can make
a bruise or break of exit for his life;   20
but is that a quietus, O tell me, is it quietus?

Surely not so! for how could murder, even self-murder
ever a quietus make?

IV

O let us talk of quiet that we know,
that we can know, the deep and lovely quiet   25
of a strong heart at peace!

How can we this, our own quietus, make?

V
Build then the ship of death, for you must take
the longest journey, to oblivion.

And die the death, the long and painful death   30
that lies between the old self and the new.

Already our bodies are fallen, bruised, badly bruised,
already our souls are oozing through the exit
of the cruel bruise.

Already the dark and endless ocean of the end   35
is washing in through the breaches of our wounds,
already the flood is upon us.

Oh build your ship of death, your little ark
and furnish it with food, with little cakes, and wine
for the dark flight down oblivion.   40

VI
Piecemeal the body dies, and the timid soul
has her footing washed away, as the dark flood rises.

We are dying, we are dying, we are all of us dying
and nothing will stay the death-flood rising within us
and soon it will rise on the world, on the outside world.   45

We are dying, we are dying, piecemeal our bodies are dying
and our strength leaves us,
and our soul cowers naked in the dark rain over the flood,
cowering in the last branches of the tree of our life.

VII
We are dying, we are dying, so all we can do   50
is now to be willing to die, and to build the ship
of death to carry the soul on the longest journey.

A little ship, with oars and food
and little dishes, and all accoutrements
fitting and ready for the departing soul.   55

Now launch the small ship, now as the body dies
and life departs, launch out, the fragile soul
in the fragile ship of courage, the ark of faith
with its store of food and little cooking pans
and change of clothes,   60
upon the flood's black waste
upon the waters of the end
upon the sea of death, where still we sail
darkly, for we cannot steer, and have no port.

There is no port, there is nowhere to go   65
only the deepening black darkening still
blacker upon the soundless, ungurgling flood
darkness at one with darkness, up and down
and sideways utterly dark, so there is no direction any more.
And the little ship is there; yet she is gone.   70
She is not seen, for there is nothing to see her by.
She is gone! gone! and yet
somewhere she is there.
Nowhere!

    VIII
And everything is gone, the body is gone   75
completely under, gone, entirely gone.
The upper darkness is heavy on the lower,
between them the little ship
is gone
she is gone.   80

It is the end, it is oblivion.

    IX
Is it illusion? or does the pallor fume
A little higher?
Ah wait, wait, for there's the dawn,
the cruel dawn of coming back to life   85
out of oblivion.

Wait, wait, the little ship
drifting, beneath the deathly ashy grey
of a flood-dawn.

Wait, wait! even so, a flush of yellow   90
and strangely, O chilled wan soul, a flush of rose.

A flush of rose, and the whole thing starts again.

  X
The flood subsides, and the body, like a worn sea-shell
emerges strange and lovely.
And the little ship wings home, faltering and lapsing   95
on the pink flood,
and the frail soul steps out, into her house again
filling the heart with peace.

Swings the heart renewed with peace
even of oblivion.   100

Oh build your ship of death, oh build it!
for you will need it.
For the voyage of oblivion awaits you.

T. S. ELIOT
1888–1965

Thomas Stearns Eliot was born in America but spent most of his adult life in England and eventually became a British citizen. He worked in London, first as a teacher and then with Lloyd's Bank, and later, after he had established himself as a major poet and influential literary critic, he became a director of the publishing firm, Faber and Faber.

Eliot is commonly thought to be, with Yeats, the greatest poet of this century. His earlier poems, which include *Preludes* and *The Love Song of J. Alfred Prufrock*, register a dissatisfaction with the squalor and spiritual emptiness of urban life which borders at times on disgust. In 1922 he published *The Waste Land*, the single most famous English poem of this century, and Eliot's most comprehensive statement about the meaninglessness of a life lived without a belief in God.

In 1927 Eliot joined the Church of England. In *Ash Wednesday* and *The Four Quartets* he meditates on the problem of coming to believe in God. These great poems are too long for this anthology, but *Journey of the Magi* in its way explores precisely this theme.

Since Eliot's poetry can be difficult to understand, it is perhaps worth remembering something he himself once said about *The Love Song of J. Alfred Prufrock*: 'as for the meaning of the poem as a whole, it is not exhausted by any single explanation, for the meaning is what the poem means to different readers.' No great poem can be reduced to a single meaning, and Eliot's poetry depends more than most on a willingness to dwell on what the various images mean to you, a willingness to reject the idea that a poem is a kind of equation which, sooner or later, can be solved. Certainly Eliot was not the avidly intellectual poet that many used to think him, and a purely intellectual approach to his poetry is not likely to yield the depths of his meaning.

Preludes

I

The winter evening settles down
With smell of steaks in passageways.
Six o'clock.
The burnt-out ends of smoky days.
And now a gusty shower wraps   5
The grimy scraps
Of withered leaves about your feet
And newspapers from vacant lots;
The showers beat
On broken blinds and chimney-pots,   10
And at the corner of the street
A lonely cab-horse steams and stamps.

And then the lighting of the lamps.

II

The morning comes to consciousness
Of faint stale smells of beer
From the sawdust-trampled street
With all its muddy feet that press
To early coffee-stands.   5

With the other masquerades
That time resumes,
One thinks of all the hands
That are raising dingy shades
In a thousand furnished rooms.   10

III

You tossed a blanket from the bed,
You lay upon your back, and waited;
You dozed, and watched the night revealing
The thousand sordid images
Of which your soul was constituted;   5
They flickered against the ceiling.
And when all the world came back
And the light crept up between the shutters
And you heard the sparrows in the gutters,
You had such a vision of the street   10
As the street hardly understands;
Sitting along the bed's edge, where
You curled the papers from your hair,
Or clasped the yellow soles of feet
In the palms of both soiled hands.   15

IV

His soul stretched tight across the skies
That fade behind a city block,
Or trampled by insistent feet
At four and five and six o'clock;
And short square fingers stuffing pipes,   5
And evening newspapers, and eyes
Assured of certain certainties,
The conscience of a blackened street
Impatient to assume the world.

I am moved by fancies that are curled   10
Around these images, and cling:
The notion of some infinitely gentle
Infinitely suffering thing.

Wipe your hand across your mouth, and laugh;
The worlds revolve like ancient women   15
Gathering fuel in vacant lots.

The Love Song of J. Alfred Prufrock

S'io credessi che mia risposta fosse
a persona che mai tornasse al mondo,
questa fiamma staria senza più scosse.
Ma per ciò che giammai di questo fondo
non tornò vivo alcun, s'i'odo il vero,
senza tema d'infamia ti rispondo.

    Let us go then, you and I,
When the evening is spread out against the sky
Like a patient etherised upon a table;
Let us go, through certain half-deserted streets,
The muttering retreats   5
Of restless nights in one-night cheap hotels
And sawdust restaurants with oyster-shells:
Streets that follow like a tedious argument
Of insidious intent
To lead you to an overwhelming question . . .   10
Oh, do not ask, 'What is it?'
Let us go and make our visit.

    In the room the women come and go
Talking of Michelangelo.

    The yellow fog that rubs its back upon the window-panes,   15
The yellow smoke that rubs its muzzle on the window-panes,
Licked its tongue into the corners of the evening,
Lingered upon the pools that stand in drains,
Let fall upon its back the soot that falls from chimneys,
Slipped by the terrace, made a sudden leap,   20
And seeing that it was a soft October night,
Curled once about the house, and fell asleep.

    And indeed there will be time
For the yellow smoke that slides along the street
Rubbing its back upon the window-panes;   25
There will be time, there will be time
To prepare a face to meet the faces that you meet;
There will be time to murder and create,
And time for all the works and days of hands

That lift and drop a question on your plate;   30
Time for you and time for me,
And time yet for a hundred indecisions,
And for a hundred visions and revisions,
Before the taking of a toast and tea.

    In the room the women come and go   35
Talking of Michelangelo.

    And indeed there will be time
To wonder, 'Do I dare?' and, 'Do I dare?'
Time to turn back and descend the stair,
With a bald spot in the middle of my hair—   40
(They will say: 'How his hair is growing thin!')
My morning coat, my collar mounting firmly to the chin,
My necktie rich and modest, but asserted by a simple pin—
(They will say: 'But how his arms and legs are thin!')
Do I dare   45
Disturb the universe?
In a minute there is time
For decisions and revisions which a minute will reverse.

    For I have known them all already, known them all—
Have known the evenings, mornings, afternoons,   50
I have measured out my life with coffee spoons;
I know the voices dying with a dying fall
Beneath the music from a farther room.
    So how should I presume?

    And I have known the eyes already, known them all—   55
The eyes that fix you in a formulated phrase,
And when I am formulated, sprawling on a pin,
When I am pinned and wriggling on the wall,
Then how should I begin
To spit out all the butt-ends of my days and ways?   60
    And how should I presume?

    And I have known the arms already, known them all –
Arms that are braceleted and white and bare
(But in the lamplight, downed with light brown hair!)

Is it perfume from a dress   65
That makes me so digress?
Arms that lie along a table, or wrap about a shawl.
   And should I then presume?
   And how should I begin?

            .   .   .   .

  Shall I say, I have gone at dusk through narrow streets   70
And watched the smoke that rises from the pipes
Of lonely men in shirt-sleeves, leaning out of windows? . . .

  I should have been a pair of ragged claws
Scuttling across the floors of silent seas.

            .   .   .   .

  And the afternoon, the evening, sleeps so peacefully!   75
Smoothed by long fingers,
Asleep . . . tired . . . or it malingers,
Stretched on the floor, here beside you and me.
Should I, after tea and cakes and ices,
Have the strength to force the moment to its crisis?   80
But though I have wept and fasted, wept and prayed,
Though I have seen my head (grown slightly bald)
   brought in upon a platter,
I am no prophet—and here's no great matter;
I have seen the moment of my greatness flicker,
And I have seen the eternal Footman hold my coat, and snicker,   85
And in short, I was afraid.

  And would it have been worth it, after all,
After the cups, the marmalade, the tea,
Among the porcelain, among some talk of you and me,
Would it have been worth while,   90
To have bitten off the matter with a smile,
To have squeezed the universe into a ball
To roll it towards some overwhelming question,
To say: 'I am Lazarus, come from the dead,
Come back to tell you all, I shall tell you all'—   95
If one, settling a pillow by her head,
   Should say: 'That is not what I meant at all.
   That is not it, at all.'

And would it have been worth it, after all,
Would it have been worth while,   100
After the sunsets and the dooryards and the sprinkled streets,
After the novels, after the teacups, after the skirts that trail
    along the floor—
And this, and so much more? –
It is impossible to say just what I mean!
But as if a magic lantern threw the nerves in patterns on a
    screen: 105
Would it have been worth while
If one, settling a pillow or throwing off a shawl,
And turning toward the window, should say:
    'That is not it at all,
    That is not what I meant, at all.'   110

     .   .   .   .   .

No! I am not Prince Hamlet, nor was meant to be;
Am an attendant lord, one that will do
To swell a progress, start a scene or two,
Advise the prince; no doubt, an easy tool,
Deferential, glad to be of use,   115
Politic, cautious, and meticulous;
Full of high sentence, but a bit obtuse;
At times, indeed, almost ridiculous—
Almost, at times, the Fool.

I grow old . . . I grow old . . .   120
I shall wear the bottoms of my trousers rolled.

Shall I part my hair behind? Do I dare to eat a peach?
I shall wear white flannel trousers, and walk upon the beach.
I have heard the mermaids singing, each to each.

I do not think that they will sing to me.   125

I have seen them riding seaward on the waves
Combing the white hair of the waves blown back
When the wind blows the water white and black.

We have lingered in the chambers of the sea
By sea-girls wreathed with seaweed red and brown   130
Till human voices wake us, and we drown.

Journey of the Magi

'A cold coming we had of it,
Just the worst time of the year
For a journey, and such a long journey:
The ways deep and the weather sharp,
The very dead of winter.'   5
And the camels galled, sore-footed, refractory,
Lying down in the melting snow.
There were times we regretted
The summer palaces on slopes, the terraces,
And the silken girls bringing sherbet.   10
Then the camel men cursing and grumbling
And running away, and wanting their liquor and women,
And the night-fires going out, and the lack of shelters,
And the cities hostile and the towns unfriendly
And the villages dirty and charging high prices: 15
A hard time we had of it.
At the end we preferred to travel all night,
Sleeping in snatches,
With the voices singing in our ears, saying
That this was all folly.   20

    Then at dawn we came down to a temperate valley,
Wet, below the snow line, smelling of vegetation,
With a running stream and a water-mill beating the darkness,
And three trees on the low sky.
And an old white horse galloped away in the meadow.   25
Then we came to a tavern with vine-leaves over the lintel,
Six hands at an open door dicing for pieces of silver,
And feet kicking the empty wine-skins.
But there was no information, and so we continued
And arrived at evening, not a moment too soon   30
Finding the place; it was (you may say) satisfactory.

    All this was a long time ago, I remember,
And I would do it again, but set down
This set down
This: were we led all that way for   35
Birth or Death? There was a Birth, certainly,
We had evidence and no doubt. I had seen birth and death,

But had thought they were different; this Birth was
Hard and bitter agony for us, like Death, our death.
We returned to our places, these Kingdoms,   40
But no longer at ease here, in the old dispensation,
With an alien people clutching their gods.
I should be glad of another death.

Marina

Quis hic locus, quae
regio, quae mundi plaga?

What seas what shores what grey rocks and what islands
What water lapping the bow
And scent of pine and the woodthrush singing through the fog
What images return
O my daughter.   5

Those who sharpen the tooth of the dog, meaning
Death
Those who glitter with the glory of the hummingbird, meaning
Death
Those who sit in the sty of contentment, meaning   10
Death
Those who suffer the ecstasy of the animals, meaning
Death

Are become unsubstantial, reduced by a wind,
A breath of pine, and the woodsong fog   15
By this grace dissolved in place

What is this face, less clear and clearer
The pulse in the arm, less strong and stronger—
Given or lent? more distant than stars and nearer than the eye

Whispers and small laughter between leaves and hurrying
    feet   20
Under sleep, where all the waters meet.

Bowsprit cracked with ice and paint cracked with heat.
I made this, I have forgotten
And remember.
The rigging weak and the canvas rotten   25
Between one June and another September.
Made this unknowing, half conscious, unknown, my own.
The garboard strake leaks, the seams need caulking.
This form, this face, this life
Living to live in a world of time beyond me; let me   30
Resign my life for this life, my speech for that unspoken,
The awakened, lips parted, the hope, the new ships.

What seas what shores what granite islands towards my
    timbers
And woodthrush calling through the fog
My daughter.   35

WILFRED OWEN
1893–1918

Wilfred Owen grew up in Shropshire. In 1911 he became a lay
assistant to the Vicar of Dunsden in Oxfordshire but, gradually, he
turned away from the Church of England, and in 1913, after a
serious illness, he took a teaching post in Bordeaux. He remained in
France until 1915 when he returned to England and enlisted in the
Artists' Rifles. After the Somme battles he was shell-shocked and
spent some time in a military hospital before returning to France. He
was awarded the Military Cross in October 1918. On the 4th
November 1918, one week before the war ended, he was killed by
machine-gun fire.

The best introduction to Owen's poetry is the Preface to the book
of war poems he was compiling shortly before he was killed:

> This book is not about heroes. English poetry is not yet fit to
> speak of them.
> Nor is it about deeds, or lands, nor anything about glory,

> honour, might, majesty, dominion, or power, except War.
> Above all I am not concerned with Poetry.
> My subject is War, and the pity of War.
> The poetry is in the pity.
> Yet these elegies are to this generation in no sense consola-
> tory. They may be to the next. All a poet can do today is warn.
> That is why true poets must be truthful. . . .

It is odd that a poet whose best verse is marked by considerable technical ingenuity should say that he is 'not concerned with Poetry'. But this comment is a reflection of his determination to reveal to his countrymen in England what the war was really like. He felt that a poet should 'warn', and, with a shocking intensity of descriptive detail, poems like *The Sentry* and *Dulce et Decorum Est* register the suffering that war inevitably involves.

A month before his death Owen wrote these words to his mother: 'My nerves are in perfect order. I came out again in order to help these boys; directly, by leading them as well as an officer can; indirectly by watching their sufferings that I may speak of them as well as a pleader can.' It is not, however, either the force of its pleading or its wealth of descriptive detail which finally disting-uishes Owen's verse from that written by other First World War poets. It is rather his depth of compassion.

Not every reader has found this compassion in Owen's poetry. The poet Yeats, for instance, refused Owen a place in the *Oxford Book of Modern Verse* on the grounds that his poetry was 'all blood and dirt'. Remember this comment of Yeats as you read the following selection, and decide, when you have thought about the poems, whether you agree with him or not.

Dulce et Decorum Est

Bent double, like old beggars under sacks,
Knock-kneed, coughing like hags, we cursed through sludge,
Till on the haunting flares we turned our backs
And towards our distant rest began to trudge.
Men marched asleep. Many had lost their boots   5
But limped on, blood-shod. All went lame; all blind;
Drunk with fatigue; deaf even to the hoots
Of tired, outstripped Five-Nines that dropped behind.

Gas! Gas! Quick, boys! – An ecstasy of fumbling,
Fitting the clumsy helmets just in time;   10
But someone still was yelling out and stumbling,
And flound'ring like a man in fire or lime . . .
Dim, through the misty panes and thick green light,
As under a green sea, I saw him drowning.

In all my dreams, before my helpless sight,   15
He plunges at me, guttering, choking, drowning.

If in some smothering dreams you too could pace
Behind the wagon that we flung him in,
And watch the white eyes writhing in his face,
His hanging face, like a devil's sick of sin;   20
If you could hear, at every jolt, the blood
Come gargling from the froth-corrupted lungs,
Obscene as cancer, bitter as the cud
Of vile, incurable sores on innocent tongues, –
My friend, you would not tell with such high zest   25
To children ardent for some desperate glory,
The old Lie: Dulce et decorum est
Pro patria mori.

The Sentry

We'd found an old Boche dug-out, and he knew,
And gave us hell; for shell on frantic shell
Lit full on top, but never quite burst through.
Rain, guttering down in waterfalls of slime,
Kept slush waist-high and rising hour by hour,   5
And choked the steps too thick with clay to climb.
What murk of air remained stank old, and sour
With fumes from whizz-bangs, and the smell of men
Who'd lived there years, and left their curse in the den,
If not their corpses . . .   10
                              There we herded from the blast
Of whizz-bangs; but one found our door at last, –
Buffeting eyes and breath, snuffing the candles,

And thud! flump! thud! down the steep steps came thumping
And sploshing in the flood, deluging muck, –
The sentry's body; then his rifle, handles   15
Of old Boche bombs, and mud in ruck on ruck.
We dredged it up, for dead, until he whined,
'O sir – my eyes, – I'm blind, – I'm blind, – I'm blind.'
Coaxing, I held a flame against his lids
And said if he could see the least blurred light   20
He was not blind; in time they'd get all right.
'I can't,' he sobbed. Eyeballs, huge-bulged like squids',
Watch my dreams still, – yet I forgot him there
In posting Next for duty, and sending a scout
To beg a stretcher somewhere, and flound'ring about   25
To other posts under the shrieking air.

Those other wretches, how they bled and spewed,
And one who would have drowned himself for good, –
I try not to remember these things now.
Let Dread hark back for one word only: how,   30
Half-listening to that sentry's moans and jumps,
And the wild chattering of his shivered teeth,
Renewed most horribly whenever crumps
Pummelled the roof and slogged the air beneath, –
Through the dense din, I say, we heard him shout   35
'I see your lights!' – But ours had long gone out.

Exposure

Our brains ache, in the merciless iced east winds that knive us . . .
Wearied we keep awake because the night is silent . . .
Low, drooping flares confuse our memory of the salient . . .
Worried by silence, sentries whisper, curious, nervous,
          But nothing happens.   5

Watching, we hear the mad gusts tugging on the wire,
Like twitching agonies of men among its brambles.
Northward, incessantly, the flickering gunnery rumbles,
Far off, like a dull rumour of some other war.
          What are we doing here?   10

The poignant misery of dawn begins to grow . . .
We only know war lasts, rain soaks, and clouds sag stormy.
Dawn massing in the east her melancholy army
Attacks once more in ranks on shivering ranks of grey,
    But nothing happens.   15

Sudden successive flights of bullets streak the silence.
Less deathly than the air that shudders black with snow,
With sidelong flowing flakes that flock, pause, and renew;
We watch them wandering up and down the wind's nonchalance,
    But nothing happens.   20

Pale flakes with fingering stealth come feeling for our faces –
We cringe in holes, back on forgotten dreams, and stare,
  snow-dazed,
Deep into grassier ditches. So we drowse, sun-dozed,
Littered with blossoms trickling where the blackbird fusses,
    – Is it that we are dying?   25

Slowly our ghosts drag home: glimpsing the sunk fires, glozed
With crusted dark-red jewels; crickets jingle there;
For hours the innocent mice rejoice: the house is theirs;
Shutters and doors, all closed: on us the doors are closed, –
    We turn back to our dying.   30

Since we believe not otherwise can kind fires burn;
Nor ever suns smile true on child, or field, or fruit.
For God's invincible spring our love is made afraid;
Therefore, not loath, we lie out here; therefore were born,
    For love of God seems dying.   35

Tonight, this frost will fasten on this mud and us,
Shrivelling many hands, puckering foreheads crisp.
The burying-party, picks and shovels in shaking grasp,
Pause over half-known faces. All their eyes are ice,
    But nothing happens.   40

Mental Cases

Who are these? Why sit they here in twilight?
Wherefore rock they, purgatorial shadows,
Drooping tongues from jaws that slob their relish,
Baring teeth that leer like skulls' teeth wicked?
Stroke on stroke of pain, – but what slow panic,   5
Gouged these chasms round their fretted sockets?
Ever from their hair and through their hands' palms
Misery swelters. Surely we have perished
Sleeping, and walk hell; but who these hellish?

– These are men whose minds the Dead have ravished.   10
Memory fingers in their hair of murders,
Multitudinous murders they once witnessed.
Wading sloughs of flesh these hapless wander,
Treading blood from lungs that had loved laughter.
Always they must see these things and hear them,   15
Batter of guns and shatter of flying muscles,
Carnage incomparable, and human squander
Rucked too thick for these men's extrication.

Therefore still their eyeballs shrink tormented
Back into their brains, because on their sense   20
Sunlight seems a blood-smear; night comes blood-black;
Dawn breaks open like a wound that bleeds afresh.
– Thus their heads wear this hilarious, hideous,
Awful falseness of set-smiling corpses.
– Thus their hands are plucking at each other;   25
Picking at the rope-knouts of their scourging;
Snatching after us who smote them, brother,
Pawing us who dealt them war and madness.

Anthem for Doomed Youth

What passing-bells for these who die as cattle?
  – Only the monstrous anger of the guns.
  Only the stuttering rifles' rapid rattle
Can patter out their hasty orisons.
No mockeries now for them; no prayers nor bells;   5
  Nor any voice of mourning save the choirs, –
The shrill, demented choirs of wailing shells;
  And bugles calling for them from sad shires.

What candles may be held to speed them all?
  Not in the hands of boys but in their eyes   10
Shall shine the holy glimmers of goodbyes.
  The pallor of girls' brows shall be their pall;
Their flowers the tenderness of patient minds,
And each slow dusk a drawing-down of blinds.

Strange Meeting

It seemed that out of battle I escaped
Down some profound dull tunnel, long since scooped
Through granites which titanic wars had groined.

Yet also there encumbered sleepers groaned,
Too fast in thought or death to be bestirred.   5
Then, as I probed them, one sprang up, and stared
With piteous recognition in fixed eyes,
Lifting distressful hands, as if to bless.
And by his smile, I knew that sullen hall, –
By his dead smile I knew we stood in Hell.   10

With a thousand pains that vision's face was grained;
Yet no blood reached there from the upper ground,
And no guns thumped, or down the flues made moan.
'Strange friend,' I said, 'here is no cause to mourn.'
'None,' said that other, 'save the undone years,   15
The hopelessness. Whatever hope is yours,

Was my life also; I went hunting wild
After the wildest beauty in the world,
Which lies not calm in eyes, or braided hair,
But mocks the steady running of the hour,   20
And if it grieves, grieves richlier than here.
For by my glee might many men have laughed,
And of my weeping something had been left,
Which must die now. I mean the truth untold,
The pity of war, the pity war distilled.   25
Now men will go content with what we spoiled,
Or, discontent, boil bloody, and be spilled.
They will be swift with swiftness of the tigress.
None will break ranks, though nations trek from progress.
Courage was mine, and I had mystery,   30
Wisdom was mine, and I had mastery:
To miss the march of this retreating world
Into vain citadels that are not walled.
Then, when much blood had clogged their chariot-wheels,
I would go up and wash them from sweet wells,   35
Even with truths that lie too deep for taint.
I would have poured my spirit without stint
But not through wounds; not on the cess of war.
Foreheads of men have bled where no wounds were.

'I am the enemy you killed, my friend.   40
I knew you in this dark: for so you frowned
Yesterday through me as you jabbed and killed.
I parried; but my hands were loath and cold.
Let us sleep now. . . .'

W. H. AUDEN
1907–1974

Wystan Hugh Auden was born in York. He went to a public school in Norfolk, and then to Oxford University where he read English Literature and began to establish his reputation as the leading poet of his generation. During the 1930s he published several collections of poetry and a number of plays. He travelled widely, living for a while in Germany, working briefly as an ambulance driver in the Spanish Civil War, and visiting Japan and China. In 1939 he emigrated to the United States and became an American citizen in 1946. He continued to spend much of his time in Europe, however, and continued to write prolifically. His last book, *Thank You, Fog*, was published posthumously in 1974, some months after he had died of a heart attack in Oxford.

Auden described the thirties as 'a time of crisis and dismay'. In Britain millions of people were unemployed, while in Germany Hitler's rise to power made the outbreak of the Second World War increasingly inevitable. It is not surprising that many of Auden's poems (*Epitaph on a Tyrant* and *Refugee Blues*, for instance) explore the social and political problems he experienced as a young man. But, as poems like *Miss Gee* and *Dear, though the night is gone* show, he was also interested in the individual human being, particularly perhaps in those he described as 'the lost, the lonely, the unhappy'.

Auden's skill as a craftsman, his ability to write poems in virtually every form is immense. He once said that a poem is 'a verbal contraption', meaning that what is important in writing poetry is not a vague inspiration but sheer intellectual mastery over rhyme, metre, and imagery. In a poem written in 1954, *The Truest Poetry is the Most Feigning*, he tells the poet who is his imaginary audience:

> Be subtle, various, ornamental, clever,
> And do not listen to those critics ever
> Whose crude provincial gullets crave in books
> Plain cooking made still plainer by plain cooks.

His own poems are far from 'plain cooking', and one of the satisfactions of reading Auden is certainly that of understanding and appreciating his control of the medium.

Auden did not, however, feel that the only justification for poetry lay in its entertainment value. 'Poetry is not concerned,' he wrote, 'with telling people what to do, but with extending our knowledge of good and evil, perhaps making the necessity for action more urgent and its nature more clear, but only leading us to the point where it is possible for us to make a rational and moral choice.' The poems in this selection pose questions about both politics and personal relationships. They might, perhaps, lead you, as Auden would have hoped, to a greater understanding of how you as an individual should act.

Miss Gee

> Let me tell you a little story
>   About Miss Edith Gee;
> She lived in Clevedon Terrace
>   At Number 83.

She'd a slight squint in her left eye,   5
 Her lips they were thin and small,
She had narrow sloping shoulders
 And she had no bust at all.

She'd a velvet hat with trimmings,
 And a dark grey serge costume;   10
She lived in Clevedon Terrace
 In a small bed-sitting room.

She'd a purple mac for wet days,
 A green umbrella too to take,
She'd a bicycle with shopping basket   15
 And a harsh back-pedal brake.

The Church of Saint Aloysius
 Was not so very far;
She did a lot of knitting,
 Knitting for that Church Bazaar.   20

Miss Gee looked up at the starlight
 And said, 'Does anyone care
That I live in Clevedon Terrace
 On one hundred pounds a year?'

She dreamed a dream one evening   25
 That she was the Queen of France
And the Vicar of Saint Aloysius
 Asked Her Majesty to dance.

But a storm blew down the palace,
 She was biking through a field of corn,   30
And a bull with the face of the Vicar
 Was charging with lowered horn.

She could feel his hot breath behind her,
 He was going to overtake;
And the bicycle went slower and slower   35
 Because of that back-pedal brake.

Summer made the trees a picture,
    Winter made them a wreck;
She bicycled to the evening service
    With her clothes buttoned up to her neck.   40

She passed by the loving couples,
    She turned her head away;
She passed by the loving couples
    And they didn't ask her to stay.

Miss Gee sat down in the side-aisle,   45
    She heard the organ play;
And the choir it sang so sweetly
    At the ending of the day,

Miss Gee knelt down in the side-aisle,
    She knelt down on her knees;   50
'Lead me not into temptation
    But make me a good girl, please.'

The days and nights went by her
    Like waves round a Cornish wreck;
She bicycled down to the doctor   55
    With her clothes buttoned up to her neck.

She bicycled down to the doctor,
    And rang the surgery bell;
'O, doctor, I've a pain inside me,
    And I don't feel very well.'   60

Doctor Thomas looked her over,
    And then he looked some more;
Walked over to his wash-basin,
    Said, 'Why didn't you come before?'

Doctor Thomas sat over his dinner,   65
    Though his wife was waiting to ring,
Rolling his bread into pellets;
    Said, 'Cancer's a funny thing.

'Nobody knows what the cause is,
   Though some pretend they do;   70
It's like some hidden assassin
   Waiting to strike at you.

'Childless women get it,
   And men when they retire;
It's as if there had to be some outlet   75
   For their foiled creative fire.'

His wife she rang for the servant,
   Said, 'Don't be so morbid, dear';
He said: 'I saw Miss Gee this evening
   And she's a goner, I fear.'   80

They took Miss Gee to the hospital,
   She lay there a total wreck,
Lay in the ward for women
   With the bedclothes right up to her neck.

They laid her on the table,   85
   The students began to laugh;
And Mr. Rose the surgeon
   He cut Miss Gee in half.

Mr. Rose he turned to his students,
   Said, 'Gentlemen, if you please,   90
We seldom see a sarcoma
   As far advanced as this.'

They took her off the table,
   They wheeled away Miss Gee
Down to another department   95
   Where they study Anatomy.

They hung her from the ceiling,
   Yes, they hung up Miss Gee;
And a couple of Oxford Groupers
   Carefully dissected her knee.   100

As I walked out one evening

As I walked out one evening,
    Walking down Bristol Street,
The crowds upon the pavement
    Were fields of harvest wheat.

And down by the brimming river   5
    I heard a lover sing
Under an arch of the railway:
    'Love has no ending.

'I'll love you, dear, I'll love you
    Till China and Africa meet,   10
And the river jumps over the mountain
    And the salmon sing in the street,

'I'll love you till the ocean
    Is folded and hung up to dry
And the seven stars go squawking   15
    Like geese about the sky.

The years shall run like rabbits,
    For in my arms I hold
The Flower of the Ages,
    And the first love of the world.'   20

But all the clocks in the city
    Began to whirr and chime:
'O let not Time deceive you,
    You cannot conquer Time.

'In the burrows of the Nightmare   25
    Where Justice naked is,
Time watches from the shadow
    And coughs when you would kiss.

'In headaches and in worry
    Vaguely life leaks away,   30
And Time will have his fancy
    To-morrow or to-day.

'Into many a green valley
    Drifts the appalling snow;
Time breaks the threaded dances   35
    And the diver's brilliant bow.

'O plunge your hands in water,
    Plunge them in up to the wrist;
Stare, stare in the basin
    And wonder what you've missed.   40

'The glacier knocks in the cupboard,
    The desert sighs in the bed,
And the crack in the tea-cup opens
    A lane to the land of the dead.

'Where the beggars raffle the banknotes   45
    And the Giant is enchanting to Jack,
And the Lily-white Boy is a Roarer,
    And Jill goes down on her back.

'O look, look in the mirror,
    O look in your distress;   50
Life remains a blessing
    Although you cannot bless.

'O stand, stand at the window
    As the tears scald and start;
You shall love your crooked neighbour   55
    With your crooked heart.'

It was late, late in the evening,
    The lovers they were gone;
The clocks had ceased their chiming,
    And the deep river ran on.   60

Dear, though the night is gone

Dear, though the night is gone,
Its dream still haunts to-day,
That brought us to a room
Cavernous, lofty as
A railway terminus,   5
And crowded in that gloom
Were beds, and we in one
In a far corner lay.

Our whisper woke no clocks,
We kissed and I was glad   10
At everything you did,
Indifferent to those
Who sat with hostile eyes
In pairs on every bed,
Arms round each other's neck,   15
Inert and vaguely sad.

What hidden worm of guilt
Or what malignant doubt
Am I the victim of,
That you then, unabashed,   20
Did what I never wished,
Confessed another love;
And I, submissive, felt
Unwanted and went out?

Lullaby

Lay your sleeping head, my love,
Human on my faithless arm;
Time and fevers burn away
Individual beauty from
Thoughtful children, and the grave   5
Proves the child ephemeral:

But in my arms till break of day
Let the living creature lie,
Mortal, guilty, but to me
The entirely beautiful.   10

Soul and body have no bounds:
To lovers as they lie upon
Her tolerant enchanted slope
In their ordinary swoon,
Grave the vision Venus sends   15
Of supernatural sympathy,
Universal love and hope;
While an abstract insight wakes
Among the glaciers and the rocks
The hermit's carnal ecstasy.   20

Certainty, fidelity
On the stroke of midnight pass
Like vibrations of a bell
And fashionable madmen raise
Their pedantic boring cry: 25
Every farthing of the cost,
All the dreaded cards foretell,
Shall be paid, but from this night
Not a whisper, not a thought,
Not a kiss nor look be lost.   30

Beauty, midnight, vision dies:
Let the winds of dawn that blow
Softly round your dreaming head
Such a day of welcome show
Eye and knocking heart may bless,   35
Find our mortal world enough;
Noons of dryness find you fed
By the involuntary powers,
Nights of insult let you pass
Watched by every human love.   40

Musée des Beaux Arts

About suffering they were never wrong,
The Old Masters: how well they understood
Its human position; how it takes place
While someone else is eating or opening a window or just
    walking dully along;
How, when the aged are reverently, passionately waiting   5
For the miraculous birth, there always must be
Children who did not specially want it to happen, skating
On a pond at the edge of the wood:
They never forgot
That even the dreadful martyrdom must run its course   10
Anyhow in a corner, some untidy spot
Where the dogs go on with their doggy life and the torturer's
    horse
Scratches its innocent behind on a tree.

In Brueghel's *Icarus*, for instance: how everything turns away
Quite leisurely from the disaster; the ploughman may   15
Have heard the splash, the forsaken cry,
But for him it was not an important failure; the sun shone
As it had to on the white legs disappearing into the green
Water; and the expensive delicate ship that must have seen
Something amazing, a boy falling out of the sky,   20
Had somewhere to get to and sailed calmly on.

Epitaph on a Tyrant

Perfection, of a kind, was what he was after,
And the poetry he invented was easy to understand;
He knew human folly like the back of his hand,
And was greatly interested in armies and fleets;
When he laughed, respectable senators burst with laughter,   5
And when he cried the little children died in the streets.

Refugee Blues

Say this city has ten million souls,
Some are living in mansions, some are living in holes:
Yet there's no place for us, my dear, yet there's no place for us.

Once we had a country and we thought it fair,
Look in the atlas and you'll find it there: 5
We cannot go there now, my dear, we cannot go there now.

In the village churchyard there grows an old yew,
Every spring it blossoms anew:
Old passports can't do that, my dear, old passports can't do
   that.

The consul banged the table and said: 10
'If you've got no passport you're officially dead':
But we are still alive, my dear, but we are still alive.

Went to a committee; they offered me a chair;
Asked me politely to return next year:
But where shall we go to-day, my dear, but where shall we go
   to-day?   15

Came to a public meeting; the speaker got up and said:
'If we let them in, they will steal our daily bread';
He was talking of you and me, my dear, he was talking of you
   and me.

Thought I heard the thunder rumbling in the sky;
It was Hitler over Europe, saying: 'They must die';   20
We were in his mind, my dear, we were in his mind.

Saw a poodle in a jacket fastened with a pin,
Saw a door opened and a cat let in:
But they weren't German Jews, my dear, but they weren't
   German Jews.

Went down the harbour and stood upon the quay,   25
Saw the fish swimming as if they were free:
Only ten feet away, my dear, only ten feet away.

Walked through a wood, saw the birds in the trees;
They had no politicians and sang at their ease:
They weren't the human race, my dear, they weren't the
   human race.   30

Dreamed I saw a building with a thousand floors,
A thousand windows and a thousand doors;
Not one of them was ours, my dear, not one of them was ours.

Stood on a great plain in the falling snow;
Ten thousand soldiers marched to and fro: 35
Looking for you and me, my dear, looking for you and me.

The Unknown Citizen

(To JS/07/M/378
This Marble Monument
Is Erected by the State)

He was found by the Bureau of Statistics to be
One against whom there was no official complaint,
And all the reports on his conduct agree
That, in the modern sense of an old-fashioned word, he was a
   saint,
For in everything he did he served the Greater Community.   5
Except for the War till the day he retired
He worked in a factory and never got fired,
But satisfied his employers, Fudge Motors Inc.
Yet he wasn't a scab or odd in his views,
For his Union reports that he paid his dues,   10
(Our report on his Union shows it was sound)
And our Social Psychology workers found
That he was popular with his mates and liked a drink.
The Press are convinced that he bought a paper every day
And that his reactions to advertisements were normal in every
   way.   15
Policies taken out in his name prove that he was fully insured,
And his Health-card shows he was once in hospital but left it
   cured.

Both Producers Research and High-Grade Living declare
He was fully sensible to the advantages of the Instalment Plan
And had everything necessary to the Modern Man,   20
A phonograph, a radio, a car and a frigidaire.
Our researchers into Public Opinion are content
That he held the proper opinions for the time of year;
When there was peace, he was for peace; when there was war,
    he went.
He was married and added five children to the population,   25
Which our Eugenist says was the right number for a parent of
    his generation,
And our teachers report that he never interfered with their
    education.
Was he free? Was he happy? The question is absurd:
Had anything been wrong, we should certainly have heard.

The Shield of Achilles

    She looked over his shoulder
        For vines and olive trees,
    Marble well-governed cities
        And ships upon untamed seas,
    But there on the shining metal   5
        His hands had put instead
    An artificial wilderness
        And a sky like lead.

A plain without a feature, bare and brown,
    No blade of grass, no sign of neighbourhood,   10
Nothing to eat and nowhere to sit down,
    Yet, congregated on its blankness, stood
    An unintelligible multitude,
A million eyes, a million boots in line,
Without expression, waiting for a sign.   15

Out of the air a voice without a face
  Proved by statistics that some cause was just
In tones as dry and level as the place:
  No one was cheered and nothing was discussed;
  Column by column in a cloud of dust   20
They marched away enduring a belief
Whose logic brought them, somewhere else, to grief.

          She looked over his shoulder
            For ritual pieties,
          White flower-garlanded heifers,   25
            Libation and sacrifice,
          But there on the shining metal
            Where the altar should have been,
          She saw by his flickering forge-light
            Quite another scene.   30

Barbed wire enclosed an arbitrary spot
  Where bored officials lounged (one cracked a joke)
And sentries sweated for the day was hot:
  A crowd of ordinary decent folk
  Watched from without and neither moved nor spoke   35
As three pale figures were led forth and bound
To three posts driven upright in the ground.

The mass and majesty of this world, all
  That carries weight and always weighs the same
Lay in the hands of others; they were small   40
  And could not hope for help and no help came:
  What their foes liked to do was done, their shame
Was all the worst could wish; they lost their pride
And died as men before their bodies died.

          She looked over his shoulder   45
            For athletes at their games,
          Men and women in a dance
            Moving their sweet limbs
          Quick, quick, to music,
            But there on the shining shield   50
          His hands had set no dancing-floor
            But a weed-choked field.

A ragged urchin, aimless and alone,
    Loitered about that vacancy, a bird
Flew up to safety from his well-aimed stone: 55
    That girls are raped, that two boys knife a third,
    Were axioms to him, who'd never heard
Of any world where promises were kept,
Or one could weep because another wept.

       The thin-lipped armourer,   60
          Hephaestos hobbled away,
       Thetis of the shining breasts
          Cried out in dismay
       At what the god had wrought
          To please her son, the strong   65
       Iron-hearted man-slaying Achilles
          Who would not live long.

PHILIP LARKIN
1922–

Philip Larkin was brought up in Coventry. As a schoolboy he tells us that he began to write 'ceaselessly . . . now verse, which I sewed up into little books, now prose, a thousand words a night after home-work.' After reading English at St John's College, Oxford, he took the first job which was offered him and became a librarian in Shropshire. Since 1955, he has been Librarian at the University of Hull. He has published four volumes of poetry and two novels.

Larkin has never married, and he has always tended to shun publicity. It was characteristic of him to remark in a radio program-me broadcast to mark his fiftieth birthday: 'I seem to have spent my life waiting for poems to turn up.' They do not in fact 'turn up' very often (he writes perhaps three or four poems a year), but enough have been published for many readers to feel that Larkin is the best poet now writing in England.

Larkin is preoccupied with what he has called 'the melancholy, the misfortunate, the frustrating, the failing elements of life'. Some readers have criticized his poetry because they find this dreariness excessive. Others feel that he should be praised for reporting honestly on what life is like in England today, and that a kind of wry, self-critical humour frequently breaks through. There is no right view in this disagreement, and you will have to work out your own reaction in the light of your experience and temperament.

What is undeniable is the technical skill with which Larkin's poems are written. Larkin has been critical of the fact that, in his view, much modern poetry is needlessly difficult, and it is easy to underestimate the craftsmanship which underlies the fluent and apparently simple movement of his own poems. A typical Larkin poem begins with a precisely observed description of a scene from contemporary life and moves to a conclusion which reflects on the significance of what has been described. He will often use colloquial language and adopt an essentially conversational style. It is, however, his mastery of traditional metrical patterns and his ability to structure his poems through the use of unobtrusive but telling rhymes which explain the extraordinary poignancy this everyday language can achieve. A poem by Larkin is as carefully wrought as any by, say, T. S. Eliot (see pages 111–120), and his technique deserves equally concentrated attention.

Wild Oats

About twenty years ago
Two girls came in where I worked—
A bosomy English rose
And her friend in specs I could talk to.
Faces in those days sparked   5
The whole shooting-match off, and I doubt
If ever one had like hers:
But it was the friend I took out,

And in seven years after that
Wrote over four hundred letters,   10
Gave a ten-guinea ring
I got back in the end, and met
At numerous cathedral cities
Unknown to the clergy. I believe

I met beautiful twice. She was trying   15
Both times (so I thought) not to laugh.

Parting, after about five
Rehearsals, was an agreement
That I was too selfish, withdrawn,
And easily bored to love.   20
Well, useful to get that learnt.
In my wallet are still two snaps
Of bosomy rose with fur gloves on.
Unlucky charms, perhaps.

Reasons for Attendance

The trumpet's voice, loud and authoritative,
Draws me a moment to the lighted glass
To watch the dancers – all under twenty-five –
Shifting intently, face to flushed face,
Solemnly on the beat of happiness.   5

– Or so I fancy, sensing the smoke and sweat,
The wonderful feel of girls. Why be out here?
But then, why be in there? Sex, yes, but what
Is sex? Surely, to think the lion's share
Of happiness is found by couples – sheer   10

Inaccuracy, as far as I'm concerned.
What calls me is that lifted, rough-tongued bell
(Art, if you like) whose individual sound
Insists I too am individual.
It speaks; I hear; others may hear as well,   15

But not for me, nor I for them; and so
With happiness. Therefore I stay outside,
Believing this; and they maul to and fro,
Believing that; and both are satisfied,
If no one has misjudged himself. Or lied.   20

Poetry of Departures

Sometimes you hear, fifth-hand,
As epitaph:
He chucked up everything
And just cleared off,
And always the voice will sound   5
Certain you approve
This audacious, purifying,
Elemental move.

And they are right, I think.
We all hate home   10
And having to be there:
I detest my room,
Its specially-chosen junk,
The good books, the good bed,
And my life, in perfect order: 15
So to hear it said

He walked out on the whole crowd
Leaves me flushed and stirred,
Like *Then she undid her dress*
Or *Take that you bastard;*   20
Surely I can, if he did?
And that helps me stay
Sober and industrious.
But I'd go today,

Yes, swagger the nut-strewn roads,   25
Crouch in the fo'c'sle
Stubbly with goodness, if
It weren't so artificial,
Such a deliberate step backwards
To create an object: 30
Books; china; a life
Reprehensibly perfect.

Church Going

Once I am sure there's nothing going on
I step inside, letting the door thud shut.
Another church: matting, seats, and stone,
And little books; sprawlings of flowers, cut
For Sunday, brownish now; some brass and stuff
Up at the holy end; the small neat organ;   5
And a tense, musty, unignorable silence,
Brewed God knows how long. Hatless, I take off
My cycle-clips in awkward reverence,

Move forward, run my hand around the font.   10
From where I stand, the roof looks almost new –
Cleaned, or restored? Someone would know: I don't.
Mounting the lectern, I peruse a few
Hectoring large-scale verses, and pronounce
'Here endeth' much more loudly than I'd meant.   15
The echoes snigger briefly. Back at the door
I sign the book, donate an Irish sixpence,
Reflect the place was not worth stopping for.

Yet stop I did: in fact I often do,
And always end much at a loss like this,   20
Wondering what to look for; wondering, too,
When churches fall completely out of use
What we shall turn them into, if we shall keep
A few cathedrals chronically on show,
Their parchment, plate and pyx in locked cases,   25
And let the rest rent-free to rain and sheep.
Shall we avoid them as unlucky places?

Or, after dark, will dubious women come
To make their children touch a particular stone;
Pick simples for a cancer; or on some   30
Advised night see walking a dead one?
Power of some sort or other will go on
In games, in riddles, seemingly at random;
But superstition, like belief, must die,
And what remains when disbelief has gone?   35
Grass, weedy pavement, brambles, buttress, sky.

A shape less recognisable each week,
A purpose more obscure. I wonder who
Will be the last, the very last, to seek
This place for what it was; one of the crew   40
That tap and jot and know what rood-lofts were?
Some ruin-bibber, randy for antique,
Or Christmas-addict, counting on a whiff
Of gown-and-bands and organ-pipes and myrrh?
Or will he be my representative,   45

Bored, uninformed, knowing the ghostly silt
Dispersed, yet tending to this cross of ground
Through suburb scrub because it held unspilt
So long and equably what since is found
Only in separation – marriage, and birth,   50
And death, and thoughts of these – for whom was built
This special shell? For, though I've no idea
What this accoutred frowsty barn is worth,
It pleases me to stand in silence here;

A serious house on serious earth it is,   55
In whose blent air all our compulsions meet,
Are recognised, and robed as destinies.
And that much never can be obsolete,
Since someone will forever be surprising
A hunger in himself to be more serious,   60
And gravitating with it to this ground,
Which, he once heard, was proper to grow wise in,
If only that so many dead lie round.

The Whitsun Weddings

That Whitsun, I was late getting away:
   Not till about
One-twenty on the sunlit Saturday
Did my three-quarters-empty train pull out,
All windows down, all cushions hot, all sense   5
Of being in a hurry gone. We ran
Behind the backs of houses, crossed a street
Of blinding windscreens, smelt the fish-dock; thence
The river's level drifting breadth began,
Where sky and Lincolnshire and water meet.   10

All afternoon, through the tall heat that slept
   For miles inland,
A slow and stopping curve southwards we kept.
Wide farms went by, short-shadowed cattle, and
Canals with floatings of industrial froth;   15
A hothouse flashed uniquely: hedges dipped
And rose: and now and then a smell of grass
Displaced the reek of buttoned carriage-cloth
Until the next town, new and nondescript,
Approached with acres of dismantled cars.   20

At first, I didn't notice what a noise
   The weddings made
Each station that we stopped at: sun destroys
The interest of what's happening in the shade,
And down the long cool platforms whoops and skirls   25
I took for porters larking with the mails,
And went on reading. Once we started, though,
We passed them, grinning and pomaded, girls
In parodies of fashion, heels and veils,
All posed irresolutely, watching us go,   30

As if out on the end of an event
   Waving goodbye
To something that survived it. Struck, I leant
More promptly out next time, more curiously,
And saw it all again in different terms: 35
The fathers with broad belts under their suits

And seamy foreheads; mothers loud and fat;
An uncle shouting smut; and then the perms,
The nylon gloves and jewellery-substitutes,
The lemons, mauves, and olive-ochres that   40

Marked off the girls unreally from the rest.
　　Yes, from cafés
And banquet-halls up yards, and bunting-dressed
Coach-party annexes, the wedding-days
Were coming to an end. All down the line   45
Fresh couples climbed aboard: the rest stood round;
The last confetti and advice were thrown,
And, as we moved, each face seemed to define
Just what it saw departing: children frowned
At something dull; fathers had never known   50

Success so huge and wholly farcical;
　　The women shared
The secret like a happy funeral;
While girls, gripping their handbags tighter, stared
At a religious wounding. Free at last,   55
And loaded with the sum of all they saw,
We hurried towards London, shuffling gouts of steam.
Now fields were building-plots, and poplars cast
Long shadows over major roads, and for
Some fifty minutes, that in time would seem   60

Just long enough to settle hats and say
　　I nearly died,
A dozen marriages got under way.
They watched the landscape, sitting side by side
– An Odeon went past, a cooling tower,   65
And someone running up to bowl – and none
Thought of the others they would never meet
Or how their lives would all contain this hour.
I thought of London spread out in the sun,
Its postal districts packed like squares of wheat: 70

There we were aimed. And as we raced across
　　Bright knots of rail
Past standing Pullmans, walls of blackened moss
Came close, and it was nearly done, this frail

Travelling coincidence; and what it held   75
Stood ready to be loosed with all the power
That being changed can give. We slowed again,
And as the tightened brakes took hold, there swelled
A sense of falling, like an arrow-shower
Sent out of sight, somewhere becoming rain.   80

Dockery and Son

'Dockery was junior to you,
Wasn't he?' said the Dean. 'His son's here now.'
Death-suited, visitant, I nod. 'And do
You keep in touch with –' Or remember how
Black-gowned, unbreakfasted, and still half-tight   5
We used to stand before that desk, to give
'Our version' of 'these incidents last night'?
I try the door of where I used to live:

Locked. The lawn spreads dazzlingly wide.
A known bell chimes. I catch my train, ignored.   10
Canal and clouds and colleges subside
Slowly from view. But Dockery, good Lord,
Anyone up today must have been born
In '43, when I was twenty-one.
If he was younger, did he get this son   15
At nineteen, twenty? Was he that withdrawn

High-collared public-schoolboy, sharing rooms
With Cartwright who was killed? Well, it just shows
How much . . . How little . . . Yawning, I suppose
I fell asleep, waking at the fumes   20
And furnace-glares of Sheffield, where I changed,
And ate an awful pie, and walked along
The platform to its end to see the ranged
Joining and parting lines reflect a strong

Unhindered moon. To have no son, no wife,   25
No house or land still seemed quite natural.
Only a numbness registered the shock

Of finding out how much had gone of life,
How widely from the others. Dockery, now:
Only nineteen, he must have taken stock   30
Of what he wanted, and been capable
Of . . . No, that's not the difference: rather, how

Convinced he was he should be added to!
Why did he think adding meant increase?
To me it was dilution. Where do these   35
Innate assumptions come from? Not from what
We think truest, or most want to do:
Those warp tight-shut, like doors. They're more a style
Our lives bring with them: habit for a while,
Suddenly they harden into all we've got   40

And how we got it; looked back on, they rear
Like sand-clouds, thick and close, embodying
For Dockery a son, for me nothing,
Nothing with all a son's harsh patronage.
Life is first boredom, then fear.   45
Whether or not we use it, it goes,
And leaves what something hidden from us chose,
And age, and then the only end of age.

The Building

Higher than the handsomest hotel
The lucent comb shows up for miles, but see,
All round it close-ribbed streets rise and fall
Like a great sigh out of the last century.
The porters are scruffy; what keep drawing up   5
At the entrance are not taxis; and in the hall
As well as creepers hangs a frightening smell.

There are paperbacks, and tea at so much a cup,
Like an airport lounge, but those who tamely sit
On rows of steel chairs turning the ripped mags   10
Haven't come far. More like a local bus.

These outdoor clothes and half-filled shopping-bags
And faces restless and resigned, although
Every few minutes comes a kind of nurse

To fetch someone away: the rest refit   15
Cups back to saucers, cough, or glance below
Seats for dropped gloves or cards. Humans, caught
On ground curiously neutral, homes and names
Suddenly in abeyance; some are young,
Some old, but most at that vague age that claims   20
The end of choice, the last of hope; and all

Here to confess that something has gone wrong.
It must be error of a serious sort,
For see how many floors it needs, how tall
It's grown by now, and how much money goes   25
In trying to correct it. See the time,
Half-past eleven on a working day,
And these picked out of it; see, as they climb

To their appointed levels, how their eyes
Go to each other, guessing; on the way   30
Someone's wheeled past, in washed-to-rags ward clothes:
They see him, too. They're quiet. To realise
This new thing held in common makes them quiet,
For past these doors are rooms, and rooms past those,
And more rooms yet, each one further off   35

And harder to return from; and who knows
Which he will see, and when? For the moment, wait,
Look down at the yard. Outside seems old enough:
Red brick, lagged pipes, and someone walking by it
Out to the car park, free. Then, past the gate,   40
Traffic; a locked church; short terraced streets
Where kids chalk games, and girls with hair-dos fetch

Their separates from the cleaners – O world,
Your loves, your chances, are beyond the stretch
Of any hand from here! And so, unreal   45
A touching dream to which we all are lulled
But wake from separately. In it, conceits

And self-protecting ignorance congeal
To carry life, collapsing only when

Called to these corridors (for now once more   50
The nurse beckons –). Each gets up and goes
At last. Some will be out by lunch, or four;
Others, not knowing it, have come to join
The unseen congregations whose white rows
Lie set apart above – women, men;   55
Old, young; crude facets of the only coin

This place accepts. All know they are going to die.
Not yet, perhaps not here, but in the end,
And somewhere like this. That is what it means,
This clean-sliced cliff; a struggle to transcend   60
The thought of dying, for unless its powers
Outbuild cathedrals nothing contravenes
The coming dark, though crowds each evening try

With wasteful, weak, propitiatory flowers.

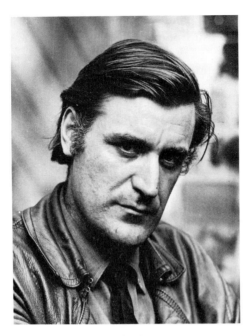

TED HUGHES
1930–

Ted Hughes was born in Yorkshire and educated at Mexborough Grammar School and Cambridge. After leaving University, he worked for brief periods as a night-watchman, a rose gardener, a reader in a film studio and as a teacher. He also travelled for a while in America. In 1956 he married the American poet, Sylvia Plath, who died in 1963. Since 1960 he has lived as a writer and farmer in Devon.

Hughes argues in *Poetry in the Making* that the secret of writing poetry successfully is to 'imagine what you are writing about. See it and live it. . . . Just look at it, touch it, smell it, listen to it, turn yourself into it.' His own poems, many of which are about animals and the natural world, are marked by this fierce concentration. We are made in *The Thought-Fox* to smell the 'sharp hot stink of fox', and in *Pike* to feel the 'hooked clamp and fangs' of the fish's jaws. Few poets have evoked creatures with such sensuous immediacy.

What interests Hughes most about the animal world is the obviousness of the struggle for survival. This is as true of the later poems, such as *Ravens*, as it is of earlier poems like *Pike*. The creatures he describes are often predators; the deaths he observes notoriously violent. Those who survive do so by virtue of their single-mindedness, and *Crow Tyrannosaurus* suggests that this is equally, for Hughes, the case with human beings. In itself this is a disturbing vision of existence. What some readers find more unsettling is the extent to which Hughes appears at times to glorify the strength and determination of the survivor to the point where he fails to sympathize with the plight of the defeated. One difference between the earlier poems and the later lies, however, in the degree to which the later poems, while continuing to present an utterly unsentimental view of life, yet explore the experience of the weak and dying with understanding and compassion. In *Ravens*, for instance, the 'piercing persistence' of the child's repeated question focusses attention on the poignancy of the lamb's still-born death, while in *The Stag* Hughes writes very much from the point of view of the hunted animal. Introducing a selection of poems from the work of the East European poet, Janos Pilinszky, Hughes wrote: 'Though the Christian culture has been stripped off so brutally, and the true condition of the animal exposed in its ugliness, and words have lost their meaning – yet out of that rise the poems, whose words are manifestly crammed with meaning'. He might equally well have been writing of his own work.

The Thought-Fox

> I imagine this midnight moment's forest:
> Something else is alive
> Beside the clock's loneliness
> And this blank page where my fingers move.
>
> Through the window I see no star: 5
> Something more near
> Though deeper within darkness
> Is entering the loneliness:
>
> Cold, delicately as the dark snow,
> A fox's nose touches twig, leaf;   10
> Two eyes serve a movement, that now
> And again now, and now, and now

Sets neat prints into the snow
Between trees, and warily a lame
Shadow lags by stump and in hollow   15
Of a body that is bold to come

Across clearings, an eye,
A widening deepening greenness,
Brilliantly, concentratedly,
Coming about its own business   20

Till, with a sudden sharp hot stink of fox
It enters the dark hole of the head.
The window is starless still; the clock ticks,
The page is printed.

Wind

This house has been far out at sea all night,
The woods crashing through darkness, the booming hills,
Winds stampeding the fields under the window
Floundering black astride and blinding wet

Till day rose; then under an orange sky   5
The hills had new places, and wind wielded
Blade-light, luminous black and emerald,
Flexing like the lens of a mad eye.

At noon I scaled along the house-side as far as
The coal-house door. I dared once to look up—   10
Through the brunt wind that dented the balls of my eyes
The tent of the hills drummed and strained its guyrope,

The fields quivering, the skyline a grimace,
At any second to bang and vanish with a flap:
The wind flung a magpie away and a black-   15
Back gull bent like an iron bar slowly. The house

Rang like some fine green goblet in the note
That any second would shatter it. Now deep
In chairs, in front of the great fire, we grip
Our hearts and cannot entertain book, thought,   20

Or each other. We watch the fire blazing,
And feel the roots of the house move, but sit on,
Seeing the window tremble to come in,
Hearing the stones cry out under the horizons.

Pike

Pike, three inches long, perfect
Pike in all parts, green tigering the gold.
Killers from the egg: the malevolent aged grin.
They dance on the surface among the flies.

Or move, stunned by their own grandeur,   5
Over a bed of emerald, silhouette
Of submarine delicacy and horror.
A hundred feet long in their world.

In ponds, under the heat-struck lily pads—
Gloom of their stillness: 10
Logged on last year's black leaves, watching upwards.
Or hung in an amber cavern of weeds

The jaws' hooked clamp and fangs
Not to be changed at this date;
A life subdued to its instrument;   15
The gills kneading quietly, and the pectorals.

Three we kept behind glass,
Jungled in weed: three inches, four,
And four and a half: fed fry to them –
Suddenly there were two. Finally one   20

With a sag belly and the grin it was born with.
And indeed they spare nobody.
Two, six pounds each, over two feet long,
High and dry and dead in the willow-herb—

One jammed past its gills down the other's gullet: 25
The outside eye stared: as a vice locks—
The same iron in this eye
Though its film shrank in death.

A pond I fished, fifty yards across,
Whose lilies and muscular tench   30
Had outlasted every visible stone
Of the monastery that planted them –

Stilled legendary depth:
It was as deep as England. It held
Pike too immense to stir, so immense and old   35
That past nightfall I dared not cast

But silently cast and fished
With the hair frozen on my head
For what might move, for what eye might move.
The still splashes on the dark pond,   40

Owls hushing the floating woods
Frail on my ear against the dream
Darkness beneath night's darkness had freed,
That rose slowly towards me, watching.

Full Moon and Little Frieda

A cool small evening shrunk to a dog bark and the clank of a
bucket—

And you listening.
A spider's web, tense for the dew's touch.
A pail lifted, still and brimming—mirror
To tempt a first star to a tremor.   5

Cows are going home in the lane there, looping the hedges
                with their warm wreaths of breath—
A dark river of blood, many boulders,
Balancing unspilled milk.

'Moon!' you cry suddenly, 'Moon! Moon!'

The moon has stepped back like an artist gazing amazed at a
                                work   10

That points at him amazed.

Crow Tyrannosaurus

Creation quaked voices—
It was a cortege
Of mourning and lament
Crow could hear and he looked around fearfully.

The swift's body fled past   5
Pulsating
With insects
And their anguish, all it had eaten.

The cat's body writhed
Gagging   10
A tunnel
Of incoming death-struggles, sorrow on sorrow.

And the dog was a bulging filterbag
Of all the deaths it had gulped for the flesh and the bones.
It could not digest their screeching finales.   15
Its shapeless cry was a blort of all those voices.

Even man he was a walking
Abattoir
Of innocents—
His brain incinerating their outcry.   20

Crow thought 'Alas
Alas ought I
To stop eating
And try to become the light?'

But his eye saw a grub. And his head, trapsprung, stabbed.   25
And he listened

And he heard
Weeping

Grubs   grubs   He stabbed   he stabbed
Weeping   30
Weeping

Weeping he walked and stabbed

Thus came the eye's
                    roundness
                              the ear's
                                        deafness.

Ravens

As we came through the gate to look at the few new lambs
On the skyline of lawn smoothness,
A raven bundled itself into air from midfield
And slid away under hard glistenings, low and guilty.
Sheep nibbling, kneeling to nibble the reluctant nibbled grass.   5
Sheep staring, their jaws pausing to think, then chewing again,
Then pausing. Over there a new lamb
Just getting up, bumping its mother's nose
As she nibbles the sugar coating off it
While the tattered banners of her triumph swing and drip
    from her rear-end.   10
She sneezes and a glim of water flashes from her rear-end.
She sneezes again and again, till she's emptied.
She carries on investigating her new present and seeing how
    it works.
Over here is something else. But you are still interested

In that new one, and its new spark of voice,   15
And its tininess.
Now over here, where the raven was,
Is what interests you next. Born dead,
Twisted like a scarf, a lamb of an hour or two,
Its insides, the various jellies and crimsons and transparencies   20
And threads and tissues pulled out
In straight lines, like tent ropes
From its upward belly opened like a lamb-wool slipper,
The fine anatomy of silvery ribs on display and the cavity,
The head also emptied through the eye-sockets,   25
The woolly limbs swathed in birth-yolk and impossible
To tell now which in all this field of quietly nibbling sheep
Was its mother. I explain
That it died being born. We should have been here, to help it.
So it died being born. 'And did it cry?' you cry.   30
I pick up the dangling greasy weight by the hooves soft as dogs'
     pads
That had trodden only womb-water
And its raven-drawn strings dangle and trail,
Its loose head joggles, and 'Did it cry?' you cry again.
Its two-fingered feet splay in their skin between the pressures   35
Of my finger and thumb. And there is another,
Just born, all black, splaying its tripod, inching its new points
Towards its mother, and testing the note
It finds in its mouth. But you have eyes now
Only for the tattered bundle of throwaway lamb.   40
'Did it cry?' you keep asking, in a three-year-old field-wide
Piercing persistence. 'Oh yes' I say 'it cried.'

Though this one was lucky insofar
As it made the attempt into a warm wind
And its first day of death was blue and warm   45
The magpies gone quiet with domestic happiness
And skylarks not worrying about anything
And the blackthorn budding confidently
And the skyline of hills, after millions of hard years,
Sitting soft.

The Stag

While the rain fell on the November woodland shoulder of
    Exmoor
While the traffic jam along the road honked and shouted
Because the farmers were parking wherever they could
And scrambling to the bank-top to stare through the tree-fringe
Which was leafless,   5
The stag ran through his private forest.

While the rain drummed on the roofs of the parked cars
And the kids inside cried and daubed their chocolate and fought
And mothers and aunts and grandmothers
Were a tangle of undoing sandwiches and screwed-round
    gossiping heads   10
Steaming up the windows,
The stag loped through his favourite valley.

While the blue horsemen down in the boggy meadow
Sodden nearly black, on sodden horses,
Spaced as at a military parade,   15
Moved a few paces to the right and a few to the left and felt
    rather foolish
Looking at the brown impassable river,
The stag came over the last hill of Exmoor.

While everybody high-kneed it to the bank-top all along the
    road
Where steady men in oilskins were stationed at binoculars,   20
And the horsemen by the river galloped anxiously this way and
    that
And the cry of hounds came tumbling invisibly with their
    echoes down through the draggle of trees,
Swinging across the wall of dark woodland,
The stag dropped into a strange country.

And turned at the river   25
Hearing the hound-pack smash the undergrowth, hearing the
    bell-note
Of the voice that carried all the others,

Then while his limbs all cried different directions to his lungs,
    which only wanted to rest,
The blue horsemen on the bank opposite
Pulled aside the camouflage of their terrible planet.   30

And the stag doubled back weeping and looking for home up a
    valley and down a valley
While the strange trees struck at him and the brambles lashed
    him,
And the strange earth came galloping after him carrying the
    loll-tongued hounds to fling all over him
And his heart became just a club beating his ribs and his own
    hooves shouted with hounds' voices,   35
And the crowd on the road got back into their cars
Wet-through and disappointed.

SEAMUS HEANEY
1939–

Seamus Heaney was born on a farm in County Derry, Northern Ireland. He studied English Literature at Queen's University, Belfast. Since graduating in 1961 he has either taught at Colleges and Universities in Ireland and America or has worked full time as a writer. He is married with three children and lives in Dublin.

Heaney is one of the most popular poets at present writing in English. His first book, *Death of a Naturalist* (1965), was notable mainly for its superb descriptions of the traditional rural activities which he remembered from his childhood. *Cow in Calf* and *At a Potato Digging* are fine examples of the power of these descriptions, although the sense of Irish history which underlies the latter poem points to the way in which Heaney has written in more recent poems about the violence which afflicts Ulster today. He is anxious, however, to avoid being cast in the role of a political poet who offers explicit commentary on the times. He wrote, for instance, in a Poetry Book Society Bulletin accompanying his collection *North*

(1975), that 'there has been considerable expectation that poets from Northern Ireland should "say" something about "the situation", but in the end they will only be worth listening to if they are saying something about and to themselves.' Poems like *Punishment* and *Casualty* certainly offer no message about what is happening in Ulster. They are more a record of how Heaney has attempted to understand the troubled society in which he lives, and to work out for himself his own position as a writer and a Catholic in that society.

The title of Seamus Heaney's second collection of poems, *Door into the Dark*, points to his belief that poems emerge from what he calls 'the buried life of the feelings'. Poetry for Heaney is a matter of 'finding a voice' so 'that you can get your own feeling into your own words and that your words have the feel of you about them'. To do this the poet needs a sure knowledge of his craft, an understanding, for instance, of rhyme, metre and imagery, but in Heaney's view there is more to the writing of poems than this kind of technical expertise. What must come first is the 'stirring of the mind round a word or an image or a memory', for, as Shakespeare puts it in a sentence Heaney is fond of quoting, 'Our poesy (poetry) is as a gum which oozes/From whence 'tis nourished'. His own poetry has been 'nourished' by his childhood experience in rural Derry, by his sense of history, and above all, perhaps, by his feeling for 'words as bearers of history and mystery'.

Digging

Between my finger and my thumb
The squat pen rests; snug as a gun.

Under my window, a clean rasping sound
When the spade sinks into gravelly ground:
My father, digging. I look down   5

Till his straining rump among the flowerbeds
Bends low, comes up twenty years away
Stooping in rhythm through potato drills
Where he was digging.

The coarse boot nestled on the lug, the shaft   10
Against the inside knee was levered firmly.
He rooted out tall tops, buried the bright edge deep
To scatter new potatoes that we picked
Loving their cool hardness in our hands.

By God, the old man could handle a spade.   15
Just like his old man.

My grandfather cut more turf in a day
Than any other man on Toner's bog.
Once I carried him milk in a bottle
Corked sloppily with paper. He straightened up   20
To drink it, then fell to right away
Nicking and slicing neatly, heaving sods
Over his shoulder, going down and down
For the good turf. Digging.

The cold smell of potato mould, the squelch and slap   25
Of soggy peat, the curt cuts of an edge
Through living roots awaken in my head.
But I've no spade to follow men like them.

Between my finger and my thumb
The squat pen rests.   30
I'll dig with it.

Follower

My father worked with a horse-plough,
His shoulders globed like a full sail strung
Between the shafts and the furrow.
The horses strained at his clicking tongue.

An expert. He would set the wing   5
And fit the bright steel-pointed sock.
The sod rolled over without breaking.
At the headrig, with a single pluck

Of reins, the sweating team turned round
And back into the land. His eye   10
Narrowed and angled at the ground,
Mapping the furrow exactly.

I stumbled in his hob-nailed wake,
Fell sometimes on the polished sod;
Sometimes he rode me on his back   15
Dipping and rising to his plod.

I wanted to grow up and plough,
To close one eye, stiffen my arm.
All I ever did was follow
In his broad shadow round the farm.   20

I was a nuisance, tripping, falling,
Yapping always. But today
It is my father who keeps stumbling
Behind me, and will not go away.

Cow in Calf

It seems she has swallowed a barrel.
From forelegs to haunches
her belly is slung like a hammock.

Slapping her out of the byre is like slapping
a great bag of seed. My hand
tingled as if strapped, but I had to
hit her again and again and
heard the blows plump like a depth-charge
far in her gut.

The udder grows. Windbags
of bagpipes are crammed there
to drone in her lowing.
Her cud and her milk, her heats and her calves
keep coming and going.

At a Potato Digging

I

A mechanical digger wrecks the drill,
Spins up a dark shower of roots and mould.
Labourers swarm in behind, stoop to fill
Wicker creels. Fingers go dead in the cold.

Like crows attacking crow-black fields, they stretch
A higgledy line from hedge to headland;
Some pairs keep breaking ragged ranks to fetch
A full creel to the pit and straighten, stand

Tall for a moment but soon stumble back
To fish a new load from the crumbled surf.
Heads bow, trunks bend, hands fumble towards the black
Mother. Processional stooping through the turf

Recurs mindlessly as autumn. Centuries
Of fear and homage to the famine god
Toughen the muscles behind their humbled knees,
Make a seasonal altar of the sod.

II

Flint-white, purple. They lie scattered
like inflated pebbles. Native
to the black hutch of clay
where the halved seed shot and clotted
these knobbed and slit-eyed tubers seem
the petrified hearts of drills. Split
by the spade, they show white as cream.

Good smells exude from crumbled earth.
The rough bark of humus erupts
knots of potatoes (a clean birth)
whose solid feel, whose wet inside
promises taste of ground and root.
To be piled in pits; live skulls, blind-eyed.

III
Live skulls, blind-eyed, balanced on   30
wild higgledy skeletons
scoured the land in 'forty-five,
wolfed the blighted root and died.

The new potato, sound as stone,
putrefied when it had lain   35
three days in the long clay pit.
Millions rotted along with it.

Mouths tightened in, eyes died hard,
faces chilled to a plucked bird.
In a million wicker huts   40
beaks of famine snipped at guts.

A people hungering from birth,
grubbing, like plants, in the bitch earth,
were grafted with a great sorrow.
Hope rotted like a marrow.   45

Stinking potatoes fouled the land,
pits turned pus into filthy mounds:
and where potato diggers are
you still smell the running sore.

IV
Under a gay flotilla of gulls   50
The rhythm deadens, the workers stop.
Brown bread and tea in bright canfuls
Are served for lunch. Dead-beat, they flop

Down in the ditch and take their fill,
Thankfully breaking timeless fasts;   55
Then, stretched on the faithless ground, spill
Libations of cold tea, scatter crusts.

Dedicatory Poem from *Wintering Out*

For David Hammond and Michael Longley

This morning from a dewy motorway   1
I saw the new camp for the internees:
a bomb had left a crater of fresh clay
in the roadside, and over in the trees

machine-gun posts defined a real stockade.   5
There was that white mist you get on a low ground
and it was déjà-vu, some film made
of Stalag 17, a bad dream with no sound.

Is there a life before death? That's chalked up
on a wall downtown. Competence with pain,   10
coherent miseries, a bite and sup,
we hug our little destiny again.

Punishment

I can feel the tug   1
of the halter at the nape
of her neck, the wind
on her naked front.

It blows her nipples   5
to amber beads,
it shakes the frail rigging
of her ribs.

I can see her drowned
body in the bog,   10
the weighing stone,
the floating rods and boughs.

Under which at first
she was a barked sapling
that is dug up   15
oak-bone, brain-firkin:

her shaved head
like a stubble of black corn,
her blindfold a soiled bandage,
her noose a ring   20

to store
the memories of love.
Little adulteress,
before they punished you

you were flaxen-haired,   25
undernourished, and your
tar-black face was beautiful.
My poor scapegoat,

I almost love you
but would have cast, I know, 30
the stones of silence.
I am the artful voyeur

of your brain's exposed
and darkened combs,
your muscles' webbing   35
and all your numbered bones:

I who have stood dumb
when your betraying sisters,
cauled in tar,
wept by the railings,   40

who would connive
in civilized outrage
yet understand the exact
and tribal, intimate revenge.

Casualty

I

He would drink by himself   1
And raise a weathered thumb
Towards the high shelf,
Calling another rum
And blackcurrant, without   5
Having to raise his voice,
Or order a quick stout
By a lifting of the eyes
And a discreet dumb-show
Of pulling off the top;   10
At closing time would go
In waders and peaked cap
Into the showery dark,
A dole-kept breadwinner
But a natural for work.   15
I loved his whole manner,
Sure-footed but too sly,
His deadpan sidling tact,
His fisherman's quick eye
And turned observant back.   20

Incomprehensible
To him, my other life.
Sometimes, on his high stool,
Too busy with his knife
At a tobacco plug   25
And not meeting my eye,
In the pause after a slug
He mentioned poetry.
We would be on our own
And, always politic   30
And shy of condescension,
I would manage by some trick
To switch the talk to eels
Or lore of the horse and cart
Or the Provisionals.   35

But my tentative art
His turned back watches too:
He was blown to bits
Out drinking in a curfew
Others obeyed, three nights   40
After they shot dead
The thirteen men in Derry.
PARAS THIRTEEN, the walls said,
BOGSIDE NIL. That Wednesday
Everybody held   45
His breath and trembled.

         II
It was a day of cold
Raw silence, wind-blown
Surplice and soutane:
Rained-on, flower-laden   50
Coffin after coffin
Seemed to float from the door
Of the packed cathedral
Like blossoms on slow water.
The common funeral   55
Unrolled its swaddling band,
Lapping, tightening
Till we were braced and bound
Like brothers in a ring.

But he would not be held   60
At home by his own crowd
Whatever threats were phoned,
Whatever black flags waved.
I see him as he turned
In that bombed offending place,   65
Remorse fused with terror
In his still knowable face,
His cornered outfaced stare
Blinding in the flash.

He had gone miles away   70
For he drank like a fish
Nightly, naturally
Swimming towards the lure

Of warm lit-up places,
The blurred mesh and murmur   75
Drifting among glasses
In the gregarious smoke.
How culpable was he
That last night when he broke
Our tribe's complicity?   80
'Now you're-supposed to be
An educated man,'
I hear him say. 'Puzzle me
The right answer to that one.'

III
I missed his funeral,   85
Those quiet walkers
And sideways talkers
Shoaling out of his lane
To the respectable
Purring of the hearse . . .   90
They move in equal pace
With the habitual
Slow consolation
Of a dawdling engine,
The line lifted, hand   95
Over fist, cold sunshine
On the water, the land
Banked under fog: that morning
I was taken in his boat,
The screw purling, turning   100
Indolent fathoms white,
I tasted freedom with him.
To get out early, haul
Steadily off the bottom,
Dispraise the catch, and smile   105
As you find a rhythm
Working you, slow mile by mile,
Into your proper haunt
Somewhere, well out, beyond . . .

Dawn-sniffing revenant,   110
Plodder through midnight rain,
Question me again.

NOTES TO POEMS

NOTES TO POEMS

WILLIAM BLAKE

Songs of Innocence

The Lamb   9

This poem was probably written for children. The first verse stresses the lamb's innocence; the second, in answer to the questions posed in the first verse, explains how God is the source of this innocence. It is interesting to compare this poem with *The Tiger* (page 18).

The Chimney Sweeper   9

3 *'weep! 'weep! 'weep! 'weep!:* this was the traditional chimney sweeper's cry, but it also suggests the sweep's unhappiness. Remember that in Blake's time chimney sweeps were small children.
8 *white hair:* 'white hair' meant fair hair at the time Blake wrote. Blake seems to have associated fair hair with innocence. The suggestion is perhaps that nothing can spoil the child's innocence.

If you read the poem aloud you will notice that the rhythm of the last three verses is different from that of the first three. What is the significance of this change?

The imagery of the poem undergoes a similar change. Consider these images in the light of the poem's meaning.

The Little Boy Lost and The Little Boy Found   10 and 11

Taken on its own, *The Little Boy Lost* seems more typical of the *Songs of Experience* than the *Songs of Innocence*. Note, though, how the last line hints at the protection which is to arrive in *The Little Boy Found*. If the actual father has failed then God is there to help. If you compare these poems with *The Little Girl Lost* and *The Little Girl Found* in the *Songs of Experience* you will see that this boy, unlike the girl in the later poems, is returned to his family.

Nurse's Song   11

The nurse in this poem is typical of the adult figures in the *Songs of Innocence* who provide the security in which children can express their joyful innocence.

Note how (3–4) the nurse herself is secure, how the play (verse 3) of the children is associated with the life of the birds and the sheep, and how night is seen, not as it is in the *Songs of Experience* as a time of danger, but simply of rest.

A Dream   12

1   *did weave a shade:* threw a shadow
3   *emmet:* ant
15   *wight:* creature

Another poem which shows how comfort is always available to creatures in distress. Note how the speaker's own bed is *angel-guarded* (2). The glow-worm and the beetle help the ant, just as angels help children.

On Another's Sorrow   12

This poem summarizes the central ideas which run through the *Songs of Innocence*.

Songs of Experience

The Clod and the Pebble   14

This poem presents two views of love. What are these two views? Consider the fact that the clod is *Trodden with the cattle's feet* (6). How does this complicate matters when you try to decide how Blake meant the reader to react to these two views? Is it possible to say the clod's view is 'good' and the pebble's 'bad'?

Some readers have felt that the clod (soft and submissive) and the pebble (hard and assertive) represent the female and male natures respectively. What is your reaction to this idea?

The Little Girl Lost   14

14   *told:* totalled

Do not worry about the meaning of the first two verses until you are familiar with the whole poem. When you *have* read the poem consider these questions. Does the tone of these verses suggest that Blake is about to make some kind of statement about how man should live? If the *desert wild* becomes a *garden mild* (7–8) then clearly some kind of radical change will have happened. Does the rest of the poem give you any idea what this change might be?

Does it seem from lines 9–18 that Lyca is in any way anxious or upset at being separated from her parents? If she is *not* anxious then what might this imply about the nature of childhood? Lines 21–28 imply that whatever Lyca might be feeling, her mother *is* anxious.

Some readers have seen *the beasts of prey* (34) as representing man's potential for violence and passion. Does this seem a possible interpretation to you? Why is it that the animals, whatever they are, protect rather than attack Lyca? What, in particular, is the implication of *hallowed* (40)?

The Little Girl Found   16

What are Lyca's parents feeling as they search for their child? What happens to them when they meet the lion, and how does the appearance of the lion seem to change? What do you take the last verse to mean?

The Tiger   18

Read the poem aloud. How would you describe its rhythm? What does this rhythm contribute to the total impact of the poem?

The word *burning* in line 1 introduces the idea of fire. What does the word suggest about the tiger? Note how the idea is continued in verse 2 and in verse 4 in the reference to the *furnace* (14).

What do you take lines 3 and 4 to mean? In the last line of the poem *Dare* is substituted for *Could*. What is the effect of this substitution?

Lines 17–18 possibly refer to the surrender of Satan and the rebel angels to God. What do you think Blake means by the question posed in line 20?

Blake's aim in this poem is clearly not so much to describe the physical characteristics of the tiger as to use the animal to pose a number of questions about life. What is it about the tiger which fascinates Blake? Do you think that the poem is as much about God as the tiger?

London   19

1 *chartered:* a charter is the formal deed by which the sovereign guarantees the rights of his subjects. It is a 'freedom', but does Blake see it in this way?
7 *ban:* curse, and prohibition
8 *mind-forged manacles:* a manacle is a hand-cuff.

Verse 1 In an earlier version Blake wrote 'dirty' instead of *chartered*. Bearing in mind the meaning of 'chartered' and what follows in the rest of the poem, which word is the more effective? Would anything be lost if the verb 'see' were substituted for *mark* in line 3? Would 'signs' be an adequate substitute for *marks* in line 4? Does the repetition of the words *chartered* and *marks* add anything to the poem?

Verse 2 Instead of *infant's cry of fear* Blake initially wrote 'voice of every child'. Which phrase do you prefer? What is the effect of the repetition of the phrase *In every*? These dreadful cries are evidence of *The mind-forged manacles* (9). Does this phrase refer to the way the lives of Londoners are ruled by a tyrannical government or to their own acceptance of their lot? Or are both ideas concentrated in the one phrase?

Verse 3 Remember that in Blake's time chimney sweepers were small children. The churches in London were becoming blackened by smoke. But Blake writes *black'ning* rather than 'blackened'. What might this suggest about his attitude to the Church? What is the attitude of the Church to the chimney sweepers? Does Blake mean that the Church is appalled or that it should be appalled by the chimney sweepers? *Appalled* could also mean 'casts a pall – a funeral cloth – over it'. It is interesting that Blake sees the soldier, too, as a victim.

Verse 4 The *plagues* of line 16 may well be venereal diseases, but Blake's main point is probably that the trouble begins with a loveless marriage, the couple entering into a living death which, perhaps, drives the husband to visit the young prostitute. This may result in his wife giving birth to a diseased child, so that a spiritual 'plague' becomes a physical one.

WILLIAM WORDSWORTH

Nutting   21

6   *wallet:* rucksack
7   *nutting-crook:* a stick to pull down the hazel branches
9   *weeds:* clothes
10 *husbanded:* kept economically
11 *exhortation:* encouragement
12 *Motley accoutrement:* patchwork clothes
30 *bower:* a shady, leafy place

In *Nutting*, as in many of his best poems, Wordsworth looks back on an incident he remembers from his childhood.

What was the boy's state of mind as he left the cottage?

Lines 14–21 describe the appearance of the hazels in the nook and the difficulty the boy had in reaching them. In the light of what is described later, is this difficult approach significant? In what kind of context would you normally expect to hear the word *devastation* (19) used? Does it seem an appropriate word for Wordsworth to use here?

Read lines 21–29 carefully. What does the word *Voluptuous* (24) suggest to you? Describe the boy's mood.

Lines 30–37 describe the *bower*, or, more exactly, how it seemed to Wordsworth as a boy. What impression of the bower do you form from this description?

Lines 43–48 describe how Wordsworth plundered the hazelnuts. Read line 44 aloud. How does the sound of the line contribute to its emotional effect? Consider the phrase *dragged to earth* in relation to what is actually being described. In the next line Wordsworth describes what he did as *merciless ravage*. Does the emotional force of this description strike you as excessive? Can you explain why Wordsworth feels and writes like this?

His reaction after stripping the tree of its nuts is complicated. Read lines 50–54 and describe this reaction.

Bearing in mind the last 4 lines (and the phrase, lines 47–48, *patiently gave up/Their quiet being*), how would you describe Wordsworth's attitude to the natural world in this poem? What, finally, would you say was the theme of the poem?

Lucy Poems   23

Strange fits of passion have I known   23

10 *lea:* meadow
25 *fond:* foolishly tender and loving
25 *wayward:* odd

What does the fact of Lucy's death add to the simile comparing her to a rose (5–6)?

The moon is first mentioned in verse 3 and appears in the next three verses. What do these references contribute to the poem?

She dwelt among the untrodden ways   24

At the heart of this poem lies the image of Lucy as *A violet by a mossy stone* (5). Define the obvious contrasts between the *violet* and the *stone*.

What is added by the adjective *mossy*? Does the violet in any sense depend on the stone? Lucy lived by the River Dove as the violet lives by the stone. What do lines 3 and 4 tell you about her life? Does she depend upon *the untrodden ways* (1) of the River Dove, and, if so, for what? The violet comparison leads (7 and 8) into the comparison of Lucy to a star. How does this new comparison affect your response to Lucy? To what extent are the two comparisons mutually contradictory?

Why in the last verse does Wordsworth choose to use the word *difference* rather than, for instance, 'sadness'?

I travelled among unknown men   24

Why does Wordsworth feel such an intense love for England?

Compare the last verse of this poem with the last verses of the previous two poems. Which of these verses seems to you to express the greatest sorrow?

A slumber did my spirit seal   25

1 *A slumber did my spirit seal:* It is difficult to pinpoint the exact meaning of this line, though line 2 perhaps helps to indicate what Wordsworth meant. A *seal* is a formal stamp, concluding an agreement, and Wordsworth certainly draws on this meaning. The implications of *seal* in the phrases 'to seal one's lips' (to bind to secrecy) and 'to seal one's fate' (to determine one's future) are also perhaps present.
7 *diurnal:* daily

Read the first verse out loud. Is 'regretful' the right word to describe Wordsworth's tone in this verse? If not, what word would you use? In answering this question you should try and decide what *human* in line 2 might mean.

In verse 2 Lucy has become *the thing* she *seemed* (3) to be when alive. What has Lucy become? The word which stands out in this verse is *diurnal* (7). Why does Wordsworth choose to use such an unusual word?

Is there any sense of loss or sadness in this poem?

Upon Westminster Bridge, September 3, 1802   25

9 *steep:* bathe

How does the fact that the first line is composed mainly of words of one syllable affect the way in which it can be read? What does the sound of the line contribute to its meaning and, therefore, to the poem as a whole?

Would you expect the word *touching* (3) to be used alongside the word *majesty*? What do you think Wordsworth means by *touching*?

What does the simile comparing the city to a *garment* (4) add to the poem?

Re-read the last four lines. What is it about the view which so affects Wordsworth?

Resolution and Independence   26

12 *plashy:* damp
43 *Chatterton:* Thomas Chatterton poisoned himself at the age of eighteen because his poems were ignored.
45 *Of Him who walked:* the Scottish poet, Burns
47 *By our own spirits are we deified:* This phrase is best understood in the light of lines 48–49. It is our *spirits* which help us to become *deified:* to lead, that is, creative, meaningful lives (literally made into gods).
80 *conned:* studied carefully
91 *sable orbs:* black eyeballs
99–100 *he had come/To gather leeches:* A leech is a blood-sucking worm. Doctors used to believe that many diseases could be cured by letting blood, and leeches were used for this purpose.

Verses I–III The poem opens with a description of nature at its happiest. What effect (18–21) does this happiness have on Wordsworth? Given the mood of the rest of the poem, why do you think Wordsworth begins the poem with these verses?

Verses IV–VII The thought of future *Solitude, pain of heart, distress, and poverty* (35) causes Wordsworth to fall into a *Dim sadness* (28). Note how in line 31 he calls himself *a happy Child of earth,* just as in line 18 he described himself *as happy as a boy.* Childhood, it seems is a happy time while *the ways of men* are *vain and melancholy* (21). Bearing this in mind, can you explain the argument of verse VI?

Verses VIII–XI The leech-gatherer is introduced into the poem. Note that there is now no reference to the happiness of nature: the leech-gatherer is met in a *lonely place* (52) near to *a pool bare to the eye of heaven* (54). He is compared in verse IX first to *a huge stone* (57) and secondly to *a sea-beast* (62). What does each of these similes add to your understanding of the leech-gatherer's appearance and existence? What impression of the leech-gatherer do you gain from verses X and XI?

Verses XII–XIV Do verses XIII and XIV in any way qualify this impression?

Verses XV–XX What do verses XVII and XX suggest about why Wordsworth is interested in the leech-gatherer? Re-read verses XV, XVIII and XIX. What is it that Wordsworth finds remarkable in his existence?

In a letter to some friends Wordsworth commented:

> I cannot conceive a figure more impressive than that of an old man like this, the survivor of a wife and ten children, travelling alone among the mountains and all lonely places, carrying with him his own fortitude. . . .

Think about this comment and your answers to the previous questions. Why do you think Wordsworth called the poem *Resolution and Independence*?

I wandered lonely as a cloud   31

16 *jocund:* cheerful

Dorothy Wordsworth described the same scene in her journal in the following manner:

> We saw a few daffodils close to the waterside. We fancied that the lake had floated the seeds ashore, and that the little colony had so sprung up. But as we went along there were more and yet more; and at last, under the boughs of the trees, we saw that there was a long belt of them along the shore, about the breadth of a country turnpike road. I never saw daffodils so beautiful. They grew among the mossy stones about and about them; some rested their heads upon these stones, as on a pillow, for weariness; and the rest tossed and reeled and danced, and seemed as if they verily laughed with the wind, that blew upon them over the lake; they looked so gay, ever glancing, ever changing.

Compare the opening four sentences of Dorothy's description with the first verse of Wordsworth's poem. In what ways are the two descriptions different? Is the opening image in the poem anything more than a piece of poetic fancy?

Dorothy makes no effort to say why she thinks the daffodils important. Wordsworth, on the other hand, devotes the last verse of his poem to an explanation of why the daffodils were significant to him. Try to explain this significance, paying particular attention to lines 21–22.

Which piece of writing do you prefer, the poem or the journal entry?

JOHN KEATS

On First Looking Into Chapman's Homer   33

Title: Homer is the Greek poet who wrote *The Odyssey* and *The Iliad*. George Chapman (1559–1634) translated Homer into English.

1   *realms of gold:* an image for Greek literature
4   *bards:* poets
    in fealty: in loyal service
    Apollo: Greek god of music and poetry
6   *demesne:* region or territory
11 *Cortez:* Spanish explorer of the sixteenth century. In fact Balboa was the first European to see the Pacific, but the mistake does not affect the poem.
14 *Darien:* the Gulf of Darien is west of the isthmus of Panama.

Keats wrote this sonnet in October 1816 after reading Chapman's translation of Homer's poetry. The opening statement *Much have I travelled in the realms of gold* introduces the central image which runs through the poem: the idea that reading an unknown poem is like discovering new *states and kingdoms* (2). Trace how this image is developed in the first eight lines. How is the image further developed in the final six lines to communicate Keats's excitement at discovering the poetry of Homer? Try to describe the emotional impact of the last three lines.

On the Sea   34

3   *Gluts:* saturates or fills
4   *Hecate:* the Queen of witches
12 *cloying:* sickly-sweet
14 *quired:* sang

The most striking phrase in the first eight lines is probably *eternal whisperings*. What are the normal associations of 'eternal' and 'whisperings'? What happens when the two words are put together? What impression of the sea do you form from the first eight lines as a whole?

Do you find the second part of the poem (9–14) as impressive as the first part?

La Belle Dame sans Merci   34

3   *sedge:* reeds or grasses
26   *manna:* manna was the food provided by God for the Israelites in
     the desert. It was said to melt when the sun rose. Here, it probably
     means delicious supernatural food.
29   *elfin grot:* fairy cave
35   *latest:* last
40   *Hath thee in thrall!:* has you as her slave
41   *gloam:* dusk
45   *sojourn:* stay

Read the poem aloud. What do the ballad form and medieval
atmosphere contribute to its over-all impact? This is a poem which can
never be tied down to a single meaning. What do you understand by
the story?

Ode to a Nightingale   36

2   *hemlock:* a poison derived from the plant of the same name
3   *opiate:* a drug containing opium
4   *Lethe-wards:* towards Lethe, the river of oblivion in Greek
     mythology
7   *Dryad:* a wood-nymph
12   *deep-delvèd:* deeply dug
13   *Flora:* the goddess of flowers
14   *Provençal:* from Provence, a region in the south of France
16   *Hippocrene:* in Greek mythology a fountain on Mount Helicon
     which was sacred to the Muses or goddesses of poetry
32   *Bacchus:* the god of wine
     pards: leopards
33   *viewless:* invisible
37   *Fays:* attendants
40   *verdurous:* greenish
43   *embalmèd darkness:* the night is heavy with 'balm' or perfume
46   *eglantine:* honeysuckle
51   *Darkling:* literally 'in the dark' but here a reference to the
     nightingale
60   *requiem:* a mass or service sung for the souls of the dead
64   *clown:* peasant
66   *sad heart of Ruth:* a reference to the Biblical story of Ruth, who, on
     the death of her husband, travelled to Bethlehem where she helped
     with the barley harvest
69   *casements:* windows
73–74 *the fancy . . . deceiving elf:* 'fancy' or the imagination, is compared
     to an elf, or fairy. The suggestion is that, like elves, the imagination
     can 'cheat' and deceive.

Verse 1 What are Keats's feelings as described in this opening verse?

Verse 2 The quick rhythms and descriptive details, *beaded bubbles winking at the brim* (17), introduce a note of elation into the poem. But the mood changes in lines 18–20. How does the sound of these final two lines establish this change of mood?

Verse 3 The mood deepens further as Keats contemplates *The weariness, the fever, and the fret* (23) of human life. Which details in this verse do you find most effective in communicating Keats's sense of human misery?

Verse 4 Keats dismisses both the morbid thoughts of the previous verse and the thought of escaping misery through alcohol (31–32). Through poetry which also makes beautiful sounds, he identifies with the nightingale (35).

Verses 5 and 6 The lush description of verse 5 with its suggestion of religion (*incense* (42)) and death (*embalmèd* (43)) leads into Keats's admission in verse 6 that he has *for many a time . . . been half in love with easeful Death* (51–2). What is it about the idea of death that he finds seductive?

Verse 7 But the thought of how the nightingale's song triumphs over time (*No hungry generations tread thee down* (62)) causes a new change of mood. How, though, should line 61 be read? Is Keats contrasting the nightingale's immortality to his own wish for death? Is his tone envious, or depressed, or what?

Verse 8 Keats emerges from the intense meditation into which the nightingale's song has led him, and wonders, in the last two lines which state is the more real: that of the meditation or that of real life.

To Autumn   38

7   *gourd:* a large, hard-rinded, fleshy fruit. The rind can be used as a bottle or a cup
11 *clammy:* moist and sticky
15 *the winnowing wind:* 'winnowing' is the name given to the activity in which corn is thrown into the air so that the wind can separate the grain from the chaff or husks
18 *swath:* a line of corn cut by a mower's sickle
19 *gleaner:* someone who collects up scraps of corn after the main harvest has been gathered in
28 *sallows:* willow trees

This is a poem in which the sounds of the words and the rhythm of the lines contribute an enormous amount to the over-all effect. Read, for instance, lines 27–33 aloud and note how the rhythm of the phrase *borne aloft/Or sinking as the light wind lives or dies* mirrors the actual movement of the gnats. It is often very difficult to say exactly what the sounds of words contribute to a poem, but read the following lines aloud and see if you can explain what is significant about the sound of the words:

Season of mists and mellow fruitfulness (1)
To bend . . . to the core (5–6)
For Summer has o'er-brimmed their clammy cells (11)
Thy hair soft-lifted by the winnowing wind (15)
While barred clouds . . . with rosy hue (25–26)

The mood of the third verse is different from that of verse 1 and 2. How would you describe this difference?

Last Sonnet   39

4 *Eremite:* hermit
6 *ablution:* ceremonial washing

Keats copied out this sonnet in his friend Severn's copy of Shakespeare when they were travelling to Italy a few months before Keats's death, but he had probably written it many months before.

The *star* (1) is seen as a hermit; the *moving waters* are *at their priest-like task* (5). Why do you think Keats introduces these religious allusions into the poem? How would you describe the over-all tone of these first eight lines?

It is the word *steadfast* (1 and 9) which links the first eight lines of the poem to the last six. What does Keats wish for in these last six lines? What is the significance of the word *No* (9) which introduces these lines?

ALFRED, LORD TENNYSON

Mariana   41

40 *marish-mosses:* marsh mosses
64 *wainscot:* wood panelling
78 *thick-moted:* a 'mote' is a particle of dust

In Shakespeare's play *Measure for Measure* Mariana is cruelly rejected by her future husband Angelo because her brother Frederick loses her dowry in a shipwreck. Tennyson's description of Mariana's isolated home matches her feelings of desolation and rejection.

In the first verse, for instance, Tennyson describes the kitchen garden of the dilapidated and lonely grange in which Mariana lives. Consider the details of this description, paying particular attention to the adjectives.

Why in the second verse do you think Tennyson uses the rather unexpected verb *trance* in line 18?

How is your understanding of her state of mind deepened in verses 3 and 6?

The poplar tree is mentioned three times in the poem, in verses 4, 5 and 7. Some readers have thought that this tree is symbolic of the man Mariana will never know. Do you feel that this interpretation is justified?

The sense of the passage of time in the poem is important in the creation of its overall impact. How does Mariana experience the passing of time? Why, in particular, does she loathe *the hour/When the thick-moted sunbeam lay/Athwart the chambers* (77–79)?

The Lady of Shalott   44

3   *wold:* open upland country
10 *aspens:* a kind of poplar, with leaves that shake in the breeze
22 *shallop:* a small boat
25 *casement:* window
56 *pad:* an easy-paced horse
76 *brazen greaves:* brass leg armour
87 *baldric:* a diagonal belt

Tennyson, like many other Romantic and Victorian poets, often drew on medieval stories and legends. Here reference is made to Camelot, the Court of King Arthur, and to Sir Lancelot who was the most famous knight in the Arthurian legends.

Part I Little is said directly about the lady. You will nevertheless form an initial impression of her as you read these verses. What is this impression, and how does it emerge?

Part II tells of how she must spend her time weaving the *magic web* (38), observing, for fear of the curse which would otherwise fall upon her, Camelot indirectly through the mirror. Do these verses develop any sense of her frustration, or does her outburst '*I am half sick of shadows*' (71) come as something of a surprise? Is it significant that it is the sight of *two young lovers* (70) which seems to provoke this outburst?

Part III What impression of Sir Lancelot do you form as you read the first four verses? Read the fifth verse carefully. How does the sentence

construction: 'She left . . ., she left . . ., She made . . ., She saw (109–112)
help communicate the lady's reaction to Lancelot?

Part IV tells of how the lady dies for her disobedience. Note how the
opening description sets an appropriate mood. The sound of the lines
also contributes a great deal to our sense of the lady's fate. How, for
instance, would you describe the tone and impact of lines 145–148?

The Victorians often complained that Tennyson's poetry was sensuous
and beautiful but lacked any real meaning. Do you feel that this poem
says anything serious about human life? Or is it a pretty fairy tale, and
no more?

Ulysses   49

3   *mete and dole:* measure and share out
6/7 *I will drink/Life to the lees:* I will drink life to the dregs
10   *Hyades:* the nymphs, who, in classical legend, formed the group of
     seven stars in the head of Taurus, the bull
17   *the ringing plains of windy Troy:* Ulysses had been one of the
     principal Greek heroes in the war against the Trojans. The Greeks
     besieged Troy to recover Helen who had eloped with Paris.
63   *Happy Isles:* the Islands of the Blest
64   *Achilles:* the greatest of the Greek soldiers, Achilles was killed
     during the siege of Troy

Tennyson wrote this poem in a single day, three weeks after he heard
the news of Arthur Hallam's death in 1833. He himself said of it that 'it
was written under the sense of loss and that all had gone by, but that
still life must be fought out to the end.' He uses the character of
Ulysses to explore his own emotional situation.

Ulysses, having wandered on many adventures around the Greek
islands and returned to his own island home of Ithaca to resume his
duties as ruler, finds that he is bored with these *common duties* (40). He
longs, once again, *To sail beyond the sunset* (60).

Why is Ulysses disenchanted with his present life? Does the adjective
idle (1) necessarily imply that he is self-critical? Look at lines 3, 4 and 5.
What do these lines reveal of his personality? What does Ulysses mean
when he says that he has *become a name* (11)? What is your attitude to
the fact that in lines 35–42 Ulysses praises his son Telemachus for
qualities which, as the opening lines show, he has no time for?

Read lines 54–70 aloud. These lines move towards the noble,
courageous assertion of the last line. This is their 'argument' or
'message'. But how would you describe the tone of these lines? Think,
in particular, about the opening sentence, and re-read, too, lines

19–21. Do you feel that there is any conflict between what Ulysses is saying and the tone of his voice? Remember, in thinking about this, that in writing the poem Tennyson was preoccupied with Hallam's death.

Is Ulysses an heroic adventurer, *strong in will* (69) or is he just *an idle king* (1)? Or is the poem more complicated than this question implies?

In Memoriam   51

Dark house, by which once more I stand   51

This, and the following two extracts, are drawn from *In Memoriam*, a long poem in four line verses written by Tennyson to express his feelings about Arthur Hallam's death.

In another of Tennyson's poems about death, *The Deserted House*, the image of the house represents a corpse. In that poem Tennyson writes:

> Close the door, the shutters close,
> Or through the windows we shall see
> The nakedness and vacancy
> Of the dark deserted house.

How does the image of the house and the street convey Tennyson's sense of despair in *Dark house*?

Besides the imagery of the house and the street, much of the poem's impact is conveyed by the rhythm which quickens in lines 3, 4 and 5. Why is this?

Read the last line of the poem out loud. What do you notice about it? Do any other lines have the same concentration of words of one syllable? What do the sounds of the words in this line convey about the poet's feelings?

With trembling fingers did we weave   51

6 *gambolled:* played
18 *meet:* fitting
25 *Rapt:* carried away
27 *keen:* fierce
    seraphic: angelic
31 *Hope:* a reference to the birth of Christ. The *light* is the star which guided the wise men to Bethlehem.

Tennyson wrote this poem at Christmas 1833. The thought of his dead friend haunts him amidst the festivities.

Read the poem aloud, thinking in particular about how the last verse should be read. Do you feel that this verse sounds a genuinely positive note? Is it a sign that Tennyson's depression might lift? Or is the tone of voice much more doubtful?

Again at Christmas did we weave   52

This poem was written the following Christmas, and is a companion to the previous one. How would you contrast the mood of this poem to that of *With trembling fingers did we weave*? Pay close attention to the way in which Tennyson has changed details in the two poems.

Tennyson said of *In Memoriam* that it was 'a very impersonal poem as well as personal'. Do these last two poems strike you as too personal and possibly sentimental in what they convey to be called impersonal expressions of feeling? Is *Dark house* a more impersonal poem?

ROBERT BROWNING

Meeting at Night   55

This poem communicates a feeling of tense excitement as the poet travels to meet his lover. How does: (a) the way each sentence is constructed and (b) the list of descriptive details contribute to this sense of tension?

Parting at Morning   56

It is the woman who is speaking in this poem. What do the last two lines suggest about her position and feelings?

A Light Woman   56

26 *basilisk:* a legendary creature with fiery, death-dealing eyes

The interest of Browning's dramatic monologues lies in the fact that his characters reveal much more than they intend. They often present a totally different and much less flattering picture of themselves than they imagine.

What is the situation or *story* (1) which lies behind this poem? What explanation does the speaker offer for his behaviour? In reading the poem you must decide whether or not you believe him.

How do you react to the way in which he describes himself as an *eagle* (15 and 21)? In thinking about this question you should note how in lines 23 and 24 he attempts to forestall any negative reaction you might have. What do verses 9 and 10 suggest both about his motives and the honesty of his account? Are you persuaded by his apparent self-criticism in line 44 or by the apparent nobility of his feelings in verse 12? How, finally, do you feel about his disregard for the woman in all he says?

Lines 53–56: Browning delays to the end the revelation that he is the hearer not the speaker.

Porphyria's Lover   58

The interest of this poem lies not so much in the simple story as in the man's motives for killing Porphyria.

Read the poem straight through so that you have an initial sense of the story. Then consider what we learn about Porphyria in the first half of the poem. Lines 21–25 are particularly important. What do you take the phrase *vainer ties* (24) to mean, and what, more generally, do these lines tell us about Porphyria's feelings and behaviour? In the light of these lines, do you feel that her earlier actions (15–20) are provocative?

Re-read lines 31–41. What are the speaker's feelings after Porphyria has told him of her love? Given these feelings, does it surprise you that he kills her? Does the phrase *Perfectly pure and good* (37) hint at an unadmitted reason for his murdering her? Lines 50–55 suggest that he believes that in killing her he has made her happy, and you may well feel that the speaker reveals here that he is mad. But before coming to any decision about these lines also consider lines 56–57. How do you think he would have spoken these lines? Happily? Regretfully? Sinisterly? Your answer to this question should deepen your understanding of the man's motives and personality.

Do you think (read in particular lines 15–30) that Porphyria is in any way to blame for what happens to her?

Browning originally published the poem under the title 'Madhouse Cells'. Do you feel that this is a better title or does it give too much away too early?

My Last Duchess   60

3   *Frà Pandolf:* an imaginary Renaissance painter
49   *munificence:* magnificent generosity
51   *dowry:* money or property brought by a bride to her husband

The speaker in this poem is a Renaissance Duke whose first wife has died. He hopes to marry the daughter of a neighbouring Count, and in this monologue is talking with the Count's envoy. As he speaks we learn a great deal both about the Duke's personality and about how he might well have been responsible for his first wife's death.

What do the words in brackets *since none puts by/The curtain I have drawn for you, but I* (9–10) suggest about the Duke?

What do lines 13–15 (*Sir, 'twas not . . . Duchess' cheek*) imply about the Duke's attitude to his first wife? How do you think he might have spoken the words *she thought* (20)?

What does the Duke disapprove of in lines 21–24? Do you feel that the Duchess is in any way at fault? What does the sentence beginning *She thanked men* (31) tell you about the reasons for the Duke's disapproval?

Is the question *Who'd stoop to blame/This sort of trifling?* (34–35) to be taken at face value? What does the verb *stoop* (repeated in lines 42 and 43) suggest to you about the Duke?

What is your reaction to lines 45–46? Has the Duke actually had his wife killed? Or is her death the result of his attitude towards her? Can we tell? Does it matter what the explanation is? Decide how he might have spoken this sentence. What does the Duke reveal about his reasons for re-marrying in the sentence beginning *I repeat* (48)?

Having talked about a portrait of his wife, he turns at the end of his speech to a statue of Neptune taming a sea-horse. Why does Browning end the poem with this detail?

Bearing in mind your answers to all of these questions, how would you describe the Duke?

A Woman's Last Word   61

Do you feel that the woman who is speaking in this poem is willing to surrender everything to the man she loves? In answering this question think carefully about the bird and animal imagery (verses 2 and 3), the references to the story of Adam and Eve (verses 4, 5 and 6), and the tone of the last 4 verses.

Two in the Campagna   63

Title *Campagna:* the plains around Rome
12 *fennel:* a yellow flowering plant
15 *weft:* threads that run in one direction in woven fabric – here meaning the spider's web
21 *champaign:* meadowland (it is the same word as Campagna)

Two lovers walk in the fields which cover the ruins of ancient Rome. The man, who is the speaker in the poem, reflects on the love he feels for his wife, and, more generally, on the nature of human love itself.

Read the poem several times to develop an initial sense of its overall meaning. Then consider verses 5, 6 and 7. The sight of the wide meadows and the natural growth of the flowers and grasses leads the speaker to suggest that the love he and his wife feel for each other should grow as naturally as the flowers do in the fields. *How is it under our control/To love or not to love?* he asks (34–35).

Now re-read verses 1–4. These verses develop a contrast between the difficulty which the speaker has in holding and understanding the *thought* which 'tantalizes' him and the natural life of the flowers and creatures which live in the fields. If you read these verses aloud you will find that the hesitant movement of the lines contributes to this sense of the speaker's difficulty. Having thought about these opening verses, do you think it is possible to accept the speaker's view as expressed in verses 6 and 7 of how human beings should relate to each other?

The remaining five verses acknowledge the difficulties inherent in all human relationships. In verse 8 the speaker wishes that his lover *were all* (36) to him, and in verse 9 that he could identify completely with her. But he is forced to recognize in verse 10 that this identification can never be complete. However passionate the embrace, *the good minute goes* (50). What does the image of the *thistle-ball* (53) in verse 11 suggest about human lives? Read the final verse carefully. The speaker's emotions change from line to line. Try to describe these changes. What do you understand by the final two lines? Do you feel that these lines summarize the theme of the whole poem?

THOMAS HARDY

Snow in the Suburbs   66

14 *inurns:* buries (the word refers to the form of burial in which a person's ashes are put into an urn)
15 *nether:* lower
17 *blanched:* whitened

Read the first verse out loud. Which words and images in this verse do you find most effective in describing the snowy scene? Think in particular about lines 5–6. Is Hardy's tone to some extent whimsical or light-hearted?

In Church   67

5 *vestry:* a small room in a church which is used for meetings and storing things

Like many of Hardy's best poems *In Church* is a marvellously economical story which focuses on a sudden moment of insight.

The Harbour Bridge   68

6 *cutwater:* the wedge-shaped end of the pier of a bridge which serves to divide the water
8 *char:* charcoal
30 *opaline:* like an opal, milky white in colour

At the heart of this poem lies the meeting between the sailor and his wife (19–28). Why does Hardy devote the first part of the poem to a description of the bridge and the people who cross it? What are your feelings on reading the last four lines?

A Trampwoman's Tragedy   69

7 *fosseway:* an old Roman road
11 *fancy-man:* sweetheart
31 *tap:* inn
49 *settle:* a long, high-backed bench

What do we learn of the trampwoman's life from the opening description of her journeys? Why do you think Hardy makes so many references in these verses to actual places?

Note how the last phrase in the first line of each verse is repeated in the second line. What is the effect of these repetitions?

Why does the trampwoman act as she does? Does Hardy blame her for her actions? How would you describe her state of mind after her lover has been executed?

Neutral Tones   72

2 *chidden:* rebuked
3 *starving:* frozen
14 *wrings with wrong:* causes undeserved suffering

White and grey are the only colours in the scene as it is described in lines 1–4. Why? How do lines 9–10 fit into this description?

What does the woman's look (5–6) say about her feelings for the man?

How successfully does Hardy communicate his feelings of despair at the relationship?

The Going   73

22–25   *Beeny Crest:* is a cliff on the North Cornish coast near the place
where Hardy met his first wife
beetling: overhanging

Hardy wrote this and the following poem, *At Castle Boterel*, after
Emma's death in November 1912. Their marriage had for many years
been unhappy, and, though they lived in the same house, they had
little to do with each other. Hardy did not even realize until too late
that his wife was dying.

Read the opening two lines of the first three verses aloud. How would
you describe the tone of the first line in each of these verses? Is this
tone modified by the second line in each verse, and if so, how?

The *perspective* (21) is literally the view down *the alley of bending boughs*
(17). But it also suggests something of what Hardy feels his future life
without Emma will be like. Consider the two phrases *darkening
dankness* (19) and *yawning blankness* (20). What does each phrase add to
your understanding of what Hardy means by the verb *sickens* (21)?

How does the mood of the poem change in the fourth verse?

Verse 5 Hardy reflects, somewhat wistfully, on how the latter years of
his marriage could have been made happier. These reflections end
abruptly at the start of the sixth verse with the words *Well, well!* (36).
How should these words be read? Sadly? Angrily? Or how?

Perhaps the most striking line in the whole poem is line 37:
Unchangeable. It must go. Note how the phrase *It must go* reflects the
title, and links back to *up and be gone* (4) and *your great going* (13). What,
though, do you understand by the word *It*? Read lines 36 and 37
aloud. Is there any difference in tone between the two lines? Read the
remaining lines aloud. What is it about the sentence *I seem but a dead
man held on end/To sink down soon . . .* (38–39) that forces you to read it
in a flat, despairing manner? How, finally, does Hardy's mood change
yet again in the final four lines, and what is it about the way in which
these lines are written that communicates his mood?

At Castle Boterel   74

  8   *chaise:* carriage
13   *balked of:* cheated of
21   *Primaeval:* ancient, going back to the beginning of the world
23   *the transitory:* things which have passed away
26   *rigour:* strictness
27   *rote:* repetition
34   *traverse:* journey across
domain: territory

Castle Boterel is the village of Boscastle in Cornwall where in March 1870 Hardy met Emma for the first time.

Do you find this a more positive and accepting poem than *The Going*? Think carefully about what is asserted in verses 3, 4 and 5. You must also try to decide, and this is very difficult, how the last verse should be read. Does the memory of youthful happiness live on, making everything else unimportant, or is the memory swamped in the last verse by Hardy's sense of his own approaching death?

The Darkling Thrush   76

  1 *coppice:* a small wood
  5 *bine-stems:* the stalks of creeping plants
  6 *lyres:* a lyre is a musical instrument like a harp
10 *outleant:* at rest. Hardy wrote this poem in 1900. He is referring in this and the following lines to the 'death' of the nineteenth century, as the year 1901 approaches.
11 *crypt:* burial-place or chapel under a church
    canopy: literally the covering over a throne or bed; here the sky
13 *germ:* seed
16 *fervourless:* lacking in warmth and happiness
20 *illimited:* unrestrained
27 *terrestrial:* earthly

How would you describe the mood of the first verse? Which details in this verse do you find most effective in establishing this mood?

What does the image of *The Century's corpse* in verse 2 add to the poem?

Why does Hardy describe the thrush as *aged . . . frail, gaunt, and small* (21)? Does this description lead you to expect the phrase *to fling his soul/Upon the growing gloom* (23–24)?

Some readers have taken the last two lines to mean that Hardy is admitting that the thrush is wiser and more courageous than he is. Others have felt that he is being ironic. How do you read these lines?

GERARD MANLEY HOPKINS

God's Grandeur   78

2 *shining:* the verb is used as a noun to convey the effect of light on
  gold foil
4 *reck his rod:* take note of his authority
6 *seared:* cut through or lacerated

A poem in which Hopkins meditates on how Nature, alive with the
presence of God, triumphs over the activities of man.

What adjectives would you use to describe the tone of the first line?
Can you find any suitable synonyms for the word *charged*? Why does
Hopkins compare *the grandeur of God* to the *ooze of oil/Crushed* in lines 4
and 5?

Re-read lines 5–8. In particular consider:
a) the effect of repeating the verb *trod* (5)
b) the force of *seared* and the internal rhymes which dominate line 6
c) the precise meaning of *smudge* (7)
What do these lines tell you about the effect which man has had on
nature, and about the strength of Hopkins's feelings?

Judging from line 8, what has been the effect of civilization upon man
himself? What do lines 12–14 tell you about Hopkins's response to
Nature and to the Holy Ghost?

Spring   79

11 *cloy:* becomes sickening
13–14 *Innocent mind . . . the winning:* Innocent youth is the most
  precious *(choice)* time of life, the time most *winning*

Consider the ways in which Hopkins describes: the *weeds* (2); the
thrush's eggs (3); the thrush's song (4–5); the *peartree* (6). In each case
try to understand the precise contribution each word makes to the
description.

Hopkins was deeply concerned in his poetry with the sounds of the
words he used, with alliteration, assonance and rhythm. What effects
does he produce by the careful selection of sounds in lines 2, 3 and 8?

Hopkins suggests in the second part of the poem that as we grow older
we lose the *Innocent mind* (13) of youth and therefore move further
away from God. The words he uses to describe this loss of innocence
are *cloy* (11), *cloud* and *sour with sinning* (12). What is the effect of the
alliteration in these lines?

Hurrahing in Harvest   79

1 *stooks:* stacked sheaves of corn or wheat
2 *wind-walks:* the paths taken by clouds as they move through the sky
3 *silk-sack:* like a silk bag which reflects the light
4 *Meal-drift:* having a texture like grain ground to powder
6 *glean:* to gather what is left on the ground after the harvest
9 *azurous:* faintly blue in colour
    world-wielding shoulder: the hills are imagined to be God's shoulders
    carrying *(wielding)* the world

In line 1 *barbarous* is a strange word to use with *beauty.* Can you explain
what Hopkins means to suggest by the phrase?

What do lines 7–8 suggest to you about Hopkins's attitude to both God
and to his fellow men?

What is the effect of seeing *These things* on the human *heart* (11–14)?
What do the repetitions contribute to the tone of the verse and,
therefore, to its meaning?

Binsey Poplars   80

1–2 *aspens:* trees similar to poplars, with leaves that shake in the
        breeze
        airy cages: the outline of the trees suggests a cage in which the
        sunlight is captured or *quelled*
6   *dandled:* moved up and down, like a baby in someone's arms
        sandalled: suggests both the criss-cross effect of the light and
        shade and also the obvious silence of the shadows
10   *delve or hew:* dig up or cut down
11   *rack:* torture
14   *sleek and seeing ball:* the eye of the next line
21   *unselve:* remove the special identity of

Binsey is an Oxford parish where Hopkins served as an assistant
priest. A row of aspens along the river bank where he used to walk
was cut down.

Hopkins suggested in a letter to a friend that his poems should be read
aloud. Read the whole poem aloud, then re-read lines 1–9 and 20–24.
What effect does he achieve in line 3? In lines 4–9? Why is *rural scene*
repeated three times in the last two lines?

Hopkins has sometimes been criticized for using eccentric and unusual
words. Here, for instance, in the phrase *dandled a sandalled shadow* (6)
the words *dandled* and *sandalled* have been chosen as much for their
sound as their meaning. Do you think this use of the words is
justified? What about *Hack and rack* (11) and *hew and delve* (18)?

How would you describe Hopkins's attitude to what man does to nature? What is it that saddens him most about the felling of these trees?

Felix Randal   81

2 *mould:* bodily build
4 *fleshed:* contained in his body
  contended: struggled together
6 *anointed:* rubbed with oil, as part of the ritual of death
  a heavenlier heart: a heart directed more towards heavenly things
7 *our sweet reprieve and ransom:* the salvation offered through Holy
  Communion
8 *all road ever:* in whatever way
9 *us:* priests
14 *fettle:* mould the shape of
  sandal: horse shoe

Felix Randal is the name the poet gives to a blacksmith or farrier in Leigh in Lancashire where Hopkins spent three months as a priest in 1879.

Re-read lines 1–4 and lines 12–14. How would you describe Hopkins's attitude to the sickness and eventual death of the blacksmith? And how, therefore, should the phrase *O is he dead then?* (1) be read? With sorrow? Or acceptance? Or how?

What do lines 5–11 tell you about Hopkins's attitude to his vocation as a priest?

No worst, there is none   81

1 *Pitched past pitch of grief:* the phrase combines the idea of being
  thrown over the edge with that of being thrown into 'pitch' or
  darkness
2 *schooled at forepangs:* as Hopkins becomes aware of his pain the
  awareness serves only to increase the pain
8 *fell:* cruel or fierce
  force: perforce
13–14 The comfort is that death will eventually end the suffering of
  life, and that each day sleep provides a relief from pain.

This poem gives expression to the sense that a gulf has developed between the poet and his 'Comforter' (the Holy Ghost) and Mary, the Mother of Jesus. It uses repetition and rhythm to convey the poet's feeling. What, for instance, is the effect of the repetition of *where* in line 3 and again in line 4? Why is *mind* repeated in line 9?

The word *herds* (5) might seem a peculiar word to apply to cries, but what does it suggest about the nature of Hopkins's sorrows? Why is *heave* applied to sorrows in the same line?

The most striking image in the poem is that of the *cliffs* of the mind (9–10). How is this image hinted at in line 1? Why is the image appropriate to the emotional experience described?

What are Hopkins's feelings at the end of the poem? Do you think, for instance, that he is able to fight against the despair that has threatened to engulf him?

W. B. YEATS

The Song of Wandering Aengus   83

Of his first meeting with Maud Gonne, Yeats wrote:

> Her complexion was luminous, like that of apple-blossom through which the light falls, and I remember her standing that first day by a great heap of such blossoms in the window.

Are there any echoes of this in the poem? What words and images do you find most important in defining the mood and experience?

He Wishes for the Cloths of Heaven   84

What part do the adjectives play in the mysterious description (1–4) of the *Cloths of Heaven*? How does the rhythm in these lines help create the desired mood? Before answering this last question read the lines aloud, noting the effect of the opening phrase: *Had I* and the way in which the adjectives and repetitions force a particular tone of voice upon the reader.

What is Yeats asking of the woman in the final three lines? How would you describe the tone of these lines? Yeats once said of this poem that it was the way to lose a lady. What do you think he meant?

Adam's Curse   84

2 *That beautiful mild woman:* Maud Gonne's sister
3 *you and I:* Yeats and Maud Gonne

Trace the way in which the poem develops from talk about poetry to an admission of defeated love. What is the central subject? What do you take the title to mean?

What similarities are there between the mood of the last ten lines and that of *He Wishes for the Cloths of Heaven*? Compare the diction of these lines to that of the earlier poem.

The Wild Swans at Coole   86

Yeats was 51 when he wrote this poem. He had first visited Coole nineteen years before. At the time of this earlier visit he was deeply depressed by his unhappy love affair with Maud Gonne. What worries him now is that it seems that he can no longer be hurt emotionally.

Read the first verse aloud. What adjectives would you use to describe the atmosphere which these lines create?

In verse 4 an implicit comparison is made between Yeats and the swans. What have the swans retained which Yeats feels he has lost?

Though the poem is perhaps more about Yeats than it is about the swans, the mystery and beauty of the swans is nevertheless important. What words and images do you find particularly effective in creating this sense of mystery?

Broken Dreams   87

1 *your hair:* Maud Gonne's
18 *The poet stubborn with his passion:* Yeats

Why is the line *Vague memories, nothing but memories* repeated three times?

Maud Gonne is now middle aged. *There is grey* in her *hair.* On the evidence of this poem has the fact of her ageing made any difference to the intensity of the love Yeats feels for her? Consider line 26 and lines 37–41. What is Yeats's attitude to his own infatuation?

The Second Coming   88

1–2 *Turning and turning . . . hear the falconer:* A *gyre* is a circular or spiral movement. The falcon circles further and further away from the falconer. In terms of the poem's argument the falcon represents man who has lost touch with Christ, or, more generally, that civilization has lost its way.
5 *blood-dimmed tide:* a tidal wave stained with blood
9–10 *Surely some revelation . . . is at hand:* the poem prophesies the coming of a new god
12 *Spiritus Mundi:* a general storehouse of images which have ceased to be the property of any personality or spirit

19   *twenty centuries:* Yeats thought that the birth of Christ ended a two thousand year cycle of civilization, and, another two thousand years having passed, that a new age was about to dawn.

The sense of the opening two lines would be retained if they were rewritten: 'The falcon cannot hear the falconer as it turns in the widening gyre.' What would be lost?

What does the image of *The blood-dimmed tide* (5) add to the idea of anarchy? What does the verb *loosed* (4) suggest to you? Why is it repeated?

The *gaze* of the beast is said to be *blank and pitiless as the sun* (15). What does this simile add to your picture of what the creature is like?

The weight of the last sentence falls heavily on the verb *Slouches* (22). Why do you think that Yeats chose this verb rather than, say, 'runs' or 'strides'? (Think of the earlier phrase *moving its slow thighs* (16).)

Which words and phrases do you find important in creating the sense of evil which haunts the poem?

A Prayer for my Daughter   89

4   *Gregory's wood:* Yeats finished the poem at Thoor Ballylee, the tower he had converted into a home near to Lady Gregory's estates in Galway

10   *the tower:* Thoor Ballylee

25   *Helen:* Helen of Troy. Yeats refers to Helen first because of her famous beauty, and, secondly, because this beauty caused her to be abducted by Paris (the *fool* of line 26). Paris's action started the Trojan war. Helen's history is, therefore, an example for Yeats of how extreme beauty can cause personal and political unhappiness.

27   *that great Queen:* Aphrodite, the Greek goddess of love, beauty and fertility, who was born from the sea

29   *bandy-leggèd smith:* Aphrodite married Hephaestos, the god of fire who was born lame; *smith* is short for 'blacksmith', a reference to Hephaestos's skill as a craftsman

32   *Horn of Plenty:* the infant Zeus gave a goat's horn to his nurse. This horn flowed with nectar and ambrosia, the drink and food of the gods. Yeats suggests that *fine women* are born possessing everything, but choose to destroy themselves through their own actions.

33   *courtesy:* not just good manners; Yeats uses the word to suggest sensitivity and delicate grace

38   *a poor man:* probably Yeats himself
41   *a flourishing hidden tree:* Yeats hopes that his daughter's life will
       develop naturally and harmoniously, *rooted*, like the *green laurel*
       in one place
59–60 *the loveliest woman born:* Maud Gonne

Written soon after the birth of his daughter, this poem defines many of
the values Yeats held most important in life.

Verses 1 and 2 The baby sleeps peacefully while the storm *is howling*
outside. Why is *scream* repeated (lines 10–11)? The wind symbolizes
the storm (see *The Second Coming*) which Yeats felt would destroy
European civilization.

Verse 3 What qualities does Yeats admire in a woman more than
beauty?

Verse 6 Do you think it is fair to say that Yeats feels that women are
happiest when occupying a passive, subservient role? Consider these
words from verse 6: *flourishing, magnanimities, merriment* and *rooted* and
make sure you understand verses 7 and 8.

EDWARD THOMAS

The Signpost   93

5–6   *traveller's-joy:* is another name for wild clematis. The *smoke* or dried
       seeds trail over the hawthorn and hazel.

On one of his long, solitary walks Thomas comes upon a signpost and
is led to reflect upon his uncertain mood.

Why is the sea described as *dim* (1)? What is the force of *glints chill*? In
what sense is the sun *shy*? Do you feel that these opening six lines
create a particular atmosphere? If so, how would you describe it?

Although line 7 can be read literally, it also hints at Thomas's
uncertainty about what he should be doing. What does the second
voice (10) state about how Thomas has felt in the past?

Read the whole of the speech of the second voice (beginning line 14)
out loud. What, according to this voice, might Thomas find to be the
flaw in *heaven* (20), and where might he find himself then wishing to
be? Does the poem end on a note of acceptance, of resignation, of
excitement, or what? How do you feel that the last two words should
be read?

March   94

Note how Thomas describes the physical onslaught of the hail, the visual impact of the sunset, and the sound of the thrushes' song.

Does the short sentence *But 'twas too late for warmth* (10) suggest anything about Thomas's own feelings?

Spring is *lost too in those mountains chill* (13–15). What does Thomas imply by the word *too*?

What is the effect of the repetition (from line 2) of *perhaps tomorrow* (32)? Are there any similarities between the ending of this poem and the last five lines of *The Signpost*?

In writing about the coming of spring is Thomas saying something about how he himself hopes to discover a new happiness? Can this be called an optimistic poem? Try and define the over-all mood created by the poem.

After Rain   95

19 *myriad:* an immense number

Which phrases in this poem strike you as particularly effective descriptions?

Beauty   96

 4 *epitaph:* an inscription on a tombstone
14 *pewit:* a lapwing (usually spelt peewit)

What does the word *it* in line 1 refer to? How should this opening question be read? With anger, resignation, sadness, or what?

The second sentence begins with a description of Thomas's emotional state and ends, heavily, on the word *now*. What would be lost if this sentence was rewritten so that its syntax was closer to that of everyday English?

Why in lines 7–10 does Thomas compare himself to an unwarmed river whose surface is cut into a pattern of fine lines by the breezes so that it resembles the pattern on the blade of a file? What associations does the word *file* have which make it more than simply a rhyme for *while*?

How does the beauty of *the misting, dim-lit, quiet vale* (13) affect Thomas? What does the bird imagery (14–16) contribute to your understanding of how his mood changes as the poem progresses? How would you describe the tone of the final three words: *Beauty is there*?

The Path   96

In this poem, as in *March*, descriptive details accumulate to define a precise visual picture while delicately suggesting a wider symbolic meaning. The path is walked by children on their way to school. Adults use the road. The children look down *the long smooth steep* (4); but the adults see only the road, the threatening wood *that overhangs/And underyawns it* (18–19), and the path itself which *looks/As if it led on to some legendary/Or fancied place where men have wished to go/And stay* (21–22).

In the light of these details, what do you think Thomas is suggesting about the difference between childhood and adulthood? Why does the path end *where the wood ends*?

October   97

4 *Harebell:* a small, bell-shaped, purple flower; *scabious* has purple flowers; *tormentil* small yellow flowers
8 *gossamers:* very fine spider threads that float in the air

Compare the poem with the passage from Thomas's *The South Country*:

> This is the beginning of the pageant of autumn, of that gradual pompous dying which has no parallel in human life, yet draws us to it with sure bonds. It is a dying of the flesh, and we see it pass through a kind of beauty which we can only call spiritual, of so high and inaccessible a strangeness is it. The sight of such perfection as is many times achieved before the end awakens the never more than lightly sleeping human desire of permanence. . . . The motion of the autumn is a fall, a surrender, requiring no effort, and therefore the mind cannot long be blind to the cycle of things as in the spring it can when the effort and delight of ascension veils the goal and the decline beyond.

Consider, for example, the poem's first nine lines in the light of the second sentence in the extract *(It is a dying . . . a strangeness is it.)*. Note how these nine lines are pre-occupied with change or *a dying of the flesh*, and how the sound and movement of the verse creates a mood very close to that defined in the prose.

Thomas's own mood as it emerges in the poem is not easy to define. Why does he want to be a part of the seasonal changes which the *earth* inevitably undergoes? Does the poem's conclusion simply assert that in retrospect this will seem *a happy day* (19), or is there a suggestion that his own personal happiness will inevitably grow out of *melancholy* (20) just as Spring will inevitably follow Autumn? (Compare *March* for a similar suggestion.)

Does *October*, in its subject matter and mood, in any way resemble *Ode to a Nightingale* and *To Autumn* by Keats (pages 36 and 38)?

As the team's head brass   98

1 *team's head brass:* the brass on the harness and the horses' heads
6 *charlock:* wild mustard, a bright yellow flower of the fields

Here Thomas explores the impact which the First World War was having on life in England. The poem begins and ends with a description of the horses ploughing the field. The rhythm of the ploughing determines the rhythm of the conversation: *One minute and an interval of ten* (16). Why does Thomas structure the poem in this way?

What does the description of the lovers, disappearing into the wood and returning from it, add to the poem?

In line 25, the ploughman tells Thomas that *one* of his *mates* is dead, killed on *The very night of the blizzard*. Earlier Thomas states that the blizzard has *felled the elm* (12). Put alongside each other, what do these two facts tell us about Thomas's attitude to the war, and, indeed, to life and death generally?

D. H. LAWRENCE

Discord in Childhood   100

This poem is built round one main image. Explain the use of the word *whips* in line 1.

What do the words *Shrieked* and *slashed* (3) suggest to you?

What is the woman's voice compared to in the second verse?

What is a *thong* (7)? Why does Lawrence use the words *booming* and *bruising* in this line?

Does this passage from the novel *Sons and Lovers* add anything which is not in the poem?

> When William was growing up, the family moved from the Bottoms to a house on the brow of the hill, commanding a view of the valley, which spread out like a convex cockle-shell, or a clamp-shell, before it. In front of the house was a huge old ash-tree. The west wind, sweeping from Derbyshire, caught the houses with full force, and the tree shrieked again. Morel liked it.

'It's music,' he said. 'It sends me to sleep.' But Paul and Arthur and
Annie hated it. To Paul it became almost a demoniacal noise. The
winter of their first year in the new house their father was very bad.
The children played in the street, on the brim of the wide, dark valley,
until eight o'clock. Then they went to bed. Their mother sat sewing
below. Having such a great space in front of the house gave the
children a feeling of night, of vastness and of terror. This terror came
in from the shrieking of the tree and the anguish of the home discord.
Often Paul would wake up, after he had been asleep a long time,
aware of thuds downstairs. Instantly he was wide awake. Then he
heard the booming shouts of his father, come home nearly drunk,
then the sharp replies of his mother, then the bang, bang of his
father's fist on the table, and the nasty, snarling shout as the man's
voice got higher. And then the whole was drowned in a piercing
medley of shrieks and cries from the great, wind-swept ash-tree. The
children lay silent in suspense, waiting for a lull in the wind to hear
what their father was doing. He might hit their mother again. There
was a feeling of horror, a kind of bristling in the darkness, and a sense
of blood. They lay with their hearts in the grip of an intense anguish.
The wind came through the tree fiercer and fiercer. All the cords of
the great harp hummed, whistled and shrieked. And then came the
horror of the sudden silence, silence everywhere, outside and
downstairs. What was it? Was it a silence of blood? What had he
done? The children lay and breathed the darkness . . .

Piano   101

10 *appassionato:* a musical term meaning 'with passion or feeling'

What effect does the woman's song have on Lawrence? Do you find
the poem nostalgic in a sentimental way? Or is Lawrence detached
from the emotion and able to write about it in a controlled way?
Consider lines 5 and 6 in particular. What does *insidious* mean, and
what is the force of *betrays*?

The Best of School   101

20 *laves:* washes

How would you define the atmosphere in the classroom as it is
described in the first thirteen lines?

The word *float* (3) introduces a sequence of images connected with
water which runs through the poem to line 20. Trace this chain of
images; what do they add to the poem?

Why exactly does Lawrence find the experience of teaching the boys so
very sweet (17)? Lawrence compares the boys to *birds* (24–25) and to
tendrils winding round a tree (29–36). Explain what each image
contributes to the poem.

Last Lesson of the Afternoon   102

15 *dross:* the scum on melted metal

If you had to read the first line out loud, what tone of voice would you use? Why does Lawrence compare the boys to a *pack of unruly hounds!* (2–5)? How is the image developed in the rest of the verse?

What are Lawrence's feelings about teaching? Compare these feelings to those expressed in *The Best of School*.

Snake   103

64 *paltry:* mean-spirited
66 *albatross:* a reference to Coleridge's poem *The Ancient Mariner* where it is the crime of killing the albatross which causes the mariner's suffering
73 *expiate:* make amends for

The snake is both an ordinary Sicilian snake and 'a mythical, god-like, lord of the underworld, an embodiment of all those dark, mysterious forces of nature which man ignobly fears or neglects'. (V. de Sola Pinto) What words and phrases in the poem suggest this god-like aspect of the snake?

The poem is as much about Lawrence's attitude to the snake as it is about the snake itself. Re-read lines 22–40 and 63–74 and try to explain the conflict which Lawrence feels as he watches the snake.

Although the language used in the poem is for the most part very simple, the mood of the poem as a whole is serious and dignified. What is it about the way in which the poem is written which explains this mood?

Bavarian Gentians   106

1 *gentians:* a blue flower of mountainous areas
2 *Michaelmas:* the festival of St Michael, September 29th
4 *Pluto:* Lord of the Underworld, home of the dead
8 *Dis:* another name for the god of the underworld
9 *Demeter:* Persephone's mother, the goddess of corn and agriculture
10 *Persephone:* daughter of Demeter and Zeus, Persephone was carried off by Pluto while picking flowers in the fields in Sicily. Pluto made her his queen, and, despite Demeter's attempts to rescue her, she was allowed to return to the earth for only six months of every year (the growing season for vegetation).

The dark blue gentians lead Lawrence to think of *Pluto's gloom* (4), and of the myth of Persephone's abduction by Pluto. Underneath these allusions lies the poet's sense of his own approaching death.

Read the poem aloud. What is the effect of the repetitions of *blue* and *dark* and of the long, flowing sentences? How would you describe the mood of this poem? Does Lawrence appear resigned to death? Does he in some way seem to welcome it? Or what?

The Ship of Death   107

17 *quietus:* a release from life (a quotation from *Hamlet,* Act III Scene I line 75, when he is contemplating suicide). The word comes from the Latin expression 'quietus est' meaning 'he is quit'. Lawrence deliberately confuses it with the word 'quiet'.

18 *bodkin:* dagger

54 *accoutrements:* equipment

In April 1927 Lawrence explored some Etruscan tombs in Italy. At one point in the book which he subsequently wrote about the Etruscan civilization, *Etruscan Places,* he describes how he saw, in the tomb of an Etruscan prince, 'the sacred treasures of the dead, the little bronze ship of death that should bear him over to the other world.' Lawrence died before he could finish the poem to his satisfaction.

Section I and II Read Section I aloud. What tone of voice best suits the words. Why does Lawrence begin the poem with references to *autumn* and *falling fruit*? The rhythm of the poem changes in the second section, and with it the tone. Try to describe these changes.

Section III and IV The question of suicide is posed and rejected. Why does Lawrence feel that suicide cannot be a satisfactory answer?

Section V Lines 30–31 introduce a new and important idea into the poem: that death means the dying of the old self and the birth of the new. Note how lines 32–34 develop the comparison between man and the *falling fruit* already begun in Section I.

Section VI It is possible to read this section, with its repetitions and powerful rhythms, in a frightened, even hysterical voice. Do you think Lawrence intended such a reading?

Sections VII and VIII These verses describe what none of us can possibly know: the actual experience of dying. How, as a poet, does Lawrence attempt this description? Is it his choice of individual words which is important? The images which he uses? The rhythm of the lines? Or what?

Sections IX and X How does Lawrence use colours in these sections to suggest the experience of re-birth?

Now try to write down what you take Lawrence's attitude to death to be as it is expressed in this poem.

T. S. ELIOT

Preludes   112

These poems are remarkable for the precise, almost cinematic, descriptive details of city life as Eliot perceived it.

I

How should line 3 be read? As a statement, a sigh? or what? What is the image in line 4?

Identify all the adjectives used in the poem. Taken together, what effect do they have?

The *cab-horse* (12) (apart from the *feet* mentioned in line 7) is the only living creature in the poem. Why is this?

How would you describe the atmosphere evoked by this poem?

II

6 *masquerades:* literally a meeting of masked people at a ball, therefore, by implication, disguises, or pretences

Again consider the cumulative effect of the adjectives.

What idea about human existence is Eliot suggesting through the use of the word *masquerades* (6)?

Suppose the word 'home' were substituted for the phrase *a thousand furnished rooms* (10). How would this alter the poem?

How would you describe Eliot's attitude to what he describes?

III

What do you take lines 5 and 6 to mean?

What do lines 14 and 15 suggest about Eliot's feelings towards this woman, and, perhaps, towards the human body in general? Does the poem show any sympathy for the woman?

IV

8 *conscience:* consciousness
9 *assume:* arrogantly to possess

What do the verbs *stretched tight* (1) and *trampled* (3) suggest about the effect of the city on the man's soul? Lines 5, 6 and 7 lead towards lines 8 and 9. The men *stuffing pipes* with their *evening newspapers* and self-confident *eyes* are the *conscience* of the *street*. Given the meaning of *assume*, what is Eliot's attitude to their *certain certainties*?

What is it that moves the poet in lines 10–13? The *soul stretched tight*, the assurance of the men, the city itself, or what?

The Love Song of J. Alfred Prufrock   114

3 *etherised:* under anaesthetic
9 *insidious:* treacherous
14 *Michelangelo:* the greatest Italian sculptor of the sixteenth century
56 *formulated phrase:* a set form of words
57 *formulated:* reduced to a formula and so denied any individuality
60 *butt-end:* cigarette end
77 *malingers:* pretends to be ill
94 *Lazarus:* friend of Jesus and brother of Martha and Mary. Jesus
    brought Lazarus back to life because his sisters were so upset at his
    death.
111 *Prince Hamlet:* the hero of Shakespeare's tragedy
115 *Deferential:* respectful, perhaps over respectful
116 *Politic:* discreet
     meticulous: scrupulously careful
117 *Full of high sentence:* impressive-sounding
     obtuse: stupid

Like Browning, Eliot is using the dramatic monologue – a poem in
which an imaginary character reveals his personality through his
preoccupations. Here J. Alfred Prufrock meditates on his failure to
declare his love to a girl he used to know, and perhaps about his
inability to make relationships. What kind of man is he and what is the
over-all mood of the poem?

The lines of Italian are taken from *The Divine Comedy*. Dante (the poet)
is visiting Hell, and these words are spoken to him by an inmate of
Hell: 'If I thought that I were answering someone who might return to
the world, this flame should shake no more. But since, if I hear truly,
no-one ever returned alive from this abyss, I have no fear of infamy
and answer you.'

Lines 1–14 tell us the time of day and the kind of town in which
Prufrock lives. How would you describe the town? What does the
adjective *overwhelming* (10) suggest about Prufrock himself? Note, too,
that the question is in fact avoided. When you have read the poem see
if you can suggest what the question might be.

What is the fog compared to in the extended simile of lines 15–22?
What does the length of the simile tell you about Prufrock? Note, too,
the equally striking simile in lines 2–3.

The word *time* appears repeatedly in lines 23–24. Why is Prufrock
preoccupied with time? Consider, in particular, lines 27 and 32–33.

In lines 37–48 Prufrock continues to dwell on the question of time as he self-consciously reflects on how other people might talk about him. Which aspects of his appearance most worry him? Do these worries seem absurd to you? Does the question posed in lines 45–46 strike you as comic in its exaggeration?

What does line 51 tell you about Prufrock's life – or at least about how he views his life? Do you find the image sad or amusing? What is the force of the verb *presume* (54, 61 and 68)? Prufrock's extreme self-consciousness again emerges in lines 55–58. How does he feel when people look at him? What does line 60 add to your understanding of his attitude to himself? How do the *arms* and *perfume* mentioned in lines 62–67 affect Prufrock?

In his loneliness Prufrock identifies himself (70–73) with the *lonely men in shirt-sleeves*. What does the image of the *ragged claws* (73) tell you about Prufrock's state of mind?

In line 82 Prufrock compares himself ironically to John the Baptist, admitting to his weakness and fear. Contemplating how his attempt to declare his love might have proceeded, he then argues himself into an acceptance of his failure to act (87–110). What does he fear might have happened if he had declared himself?

What do the references to *Hamlet* (111–119) add to your understanding of Prufrock's personality? How should lines 120–125 be read? Self-pityingly? With self-conscious humour? Or how?

What does the image of the mermaids tell you about Prufrock's state of mind? How does the image affect you emotionally? Do you feel that Eliot has presented Prufrock's personality and predicament successfully? Are you left with feelings of sympathy for Prufrock, or what?

Journey of the Magi   118

The Magi were the three wise men who visited the infant Christ in Bethlehem.

 6 *refractory:* obstinate
10 *sherbet:* here a cool drink
26 *lintel:* the stone over a doorway
41 *dispensation:* religious system or order

The poem, which is spoken by one of the Magi many years after his journey (see line 33), describes the circumstances of the journey (verses 1 and 2) and reflects (verse 3) on the significance of the experience.

What do lines 8–10 suggest about the kind of life the Magi enjoyed prior to visiting Bethlehem? What kinds of things made the journey difficult? Is it significant that the first verse ends with lines 19–20?

How does the *temperate valley* (21) differ from the lands they have passed through earlier on the journey?

What events which were later to happen in Christ's life are suggested by lines 24 and 27?

The second verse ends on a deliberately off-hand note. This understatement, the contrast between the significance of what is described and the tone of the description, is a notable feature of the poem. What does it add to the poem?

The end of the poem reflects on the question posed in lines 35–36. The *Birth* is obviously that of Christ. Why, though, does the 'speaker' see the experience as a kind of *Death*? (38–39).

What is it (lines 41–42) that makes life on return to his country difficult? What is he now looking forward to?

It is interesting to compare this poem with Yeats's *The Second Coming* (page 88).

Marina   119

The title derives from Shakespeare's play *Pericles*, in which Pericles is saved from despair by his daughter, Marina, who he thought was lost.

Epigraph: 'What place is this? What region? What quarter of the world?' Hercules, in the play *Hercules Furens* by the Latin poet Seneca, kills his family while in a fit of madness. After the murders he falls asleep, and, on waking, gradually realizes where he is and what he has done. The speaker in this poem is in a similar state of awakening, though, unlike Hercules, he awakens to a growing sense of hope. Taken together, the title and the epigraph provide the context for the poem itself.

22 *bowsprit:* the pole which projects over the bows of a ship
28 *garboard strake:* the first range of planks laid on the bottom of a ship next to the keel
   cauling: making water-tight

Lines 6–13 hint at different vices or forms of spiritual death: the *tooth* of gluttony, the *glory* of pride, the *sty* of sloth, and *ecstasy* of lust. But these images have *become unsubstantial*: defeated by the sense of *grace* associated with Marina. What do you understand the word 'grace' to mean?

The speaker (16–21) is still in a state of awakening and is unsure what the images can mean.

The central image in lines 22–32 is that of the boat. What does the poor condition of the boat imply about the speaker's life? What does he hope for in lines 30–33?

Note that the woodthrush is now *calling through the fog* (34) where in line 3 it was merely *singing*. There is still the fog to sail through, but there is, it seems, the possibility of hope and guidance.

WILFRED OWEN

Dulce et Decorum Est   122

The title ('It is a sweet and seemly thing to die for one's country) is a quotation from the Latin poet, Horace.

  8 *Five-Nines:* gas shells
23 *cud:* food brought back from the first stomach of an animal like a cow to be chewed again
26 *ardent:* burning

Why does Owen compare the soldiers to *old beggars* (1) and *hags* (2)? In answering this question remember that children are mentioned in line 26.

Read lines 5, 6 and 7 out loud. Many of the words are of only one syllable. The sentences are, moreover, short. What effect does this have on the way in which you can read these lines? Compare them to lines 9–12. In what way is the rhythm of these lines different from that of the earlier lines? Explain this difference in terms of what is happening to the soldiers.

The last verse of the poem forms one long sentence. This sentence divides into three sections, the two clauses which begin with the word *If* and the concluding statement which begins *My friend*. The vocabulary and images of the first two sections are intense and, at times, repulsive. Why? Consider in particular the force of *smothering* (17), *flung* (18), *writhing* (19), and *gargling* (22). How would you describe the language of the last section? Read the whole verse out loud to help you to decide how these lines develop and finally deliver their argument.

What do you think Owen meant by giving the poem such a title?

The Sentry   123

1 *Boche:* German
8 *whizz-bangs* and 34 *crumps:* slang for the blast and noise of shells

The immediate horror described here is obviously the blinding of the soldier. At the heart of the poem, however, lies the dilemma of the young officer who is powerless to help his wounded men. Owen was such an officer, and the poem describes an incident which happened to him.

Read line 2 out loud. Why does Owen use words of one syllable? What is the effect of the internal rhyme *hell* with *shell*? Why does Owen use the word *guttering* in line 4?

Read line 6 aloud. What does the sound of the words contribute to the description?

If you substituted 'sheltered' for the verb *herded* in line 10 what would be lost from the poem?

13–15: The subject of the sentence *(The sentry's body)* is delayed until the end of the sentence. Why?

An alternative version of line 17 reads: 'We dredged him up, for killed, until he whined'. Which version do you prefer? What is the force of the verb *dredged*?

Exposure   124

3 *the salient:* the point where the system of trenches juts out
26 *glozed:* brightened

This extract from a letter Owen wrote in 1917 describes the experiences which led him to write *Exposure*:

> In this place my platoon had no dug-outs, but had to lie in the snow under the deadly wind. By day it was impossible to stand up, or even crawl about because we were behind only a little ridge screening us from the Boche's periscope. We had five Tommy's cookers between the platoon, but they did not suffice to melt the ice in the water-cans. So we suffered cruelly from thirst. The marvel is that we did not all die of cold. As a matter of fact, only one of my party actually froze to death. . . .

In lines 13–15 the dawn clouds are visualized in terms of the German troops (who wore grey uniforms). This metaphor provides a striking description of dawn. But what does it tell you about the soldiers' state of mind? Consider in particular the words *massing, melancholy, Attacks* and *shivering*.

The exhausted and freezing soldiers dream of the warmth of summer (verse 5) and the security of home (verse 6). Compare the language to that used in the rest of the poem. How effectively do these verses evoke a different world?

Consider the short lines which end each verse. Taken together, what do they tell you about the soldiers' feelings?

Earlier editions print line 36: 'Tonight, His frost will fasten on this mud and us'. What difference does it make to the meaning to replace 'His' with 'this'?

Mental Cases   126

2 *purgatorial shadows:* purgatory is the place where, after death, souls are purified from sin, according to Roman Catholic doctrine
6 *fretted sockets:* worried and deeply sunken eyes
12 *Multitudinous:* huge numbers of
13 *sloughs:* hollows; perhaps an image of the mud of No-man's land, littered with corpses
17–18 *human squander . . . extrication:* human bodies stacked too deeply and wastefully for these men ever to set themselves free from the memory
26 *knout:* whip

What impression of the 'mental cases' do you form from the first verse? How would you define Owen's attitude to these men? Does his attitude change from verse to verse? How do lines 27–28 help you to understand his feelings?

Anthem for Doomed Youth   127

1 *passing-bells:* the bells which are rung when someone dies
4 *orisons:* prayers
8 *shires:* counties
9 *speed:* send them on their way to Heaven
12 *pall:* the cloth which is draped over a coffin
14 *a drawing-down of blinds:* to draw down the blinds is a mark of respect for the dead

How should the first line be read? Angrily? Sarcastically? Sadly? Or how? Read lines 2 and 3 aloud. How does the sound of each of these lines fit what is being described?

Why are *wailing shells* described as *shrill, demented choirs* (7)?

9–14: Since these young soldiers have died in battle, they cannot have a proper funeral. Their only memorial is the sad patience of those they have left behind. How does the mood of this verse differ from that of the first?

Strange Meeting   127

3 *Through granites . . . groined:* a 'groin' is an architectural term meaning the line of intersection of two vaults. The granite is seen as a vast building created by *titanic* or gigantic geological forces.

38 *cess:* an abbreviated form of 'cess-pit', a pit for collecting foul water and sewage

The narrator has been killed in battle. He awakes to find himself in Hell where he talks with *the enemy* (40) he had killed the previous day. It has been suggested that this enemy is as much an aspect of Owen's personality as he is a German soldier-poet. His sense of the sad wastefulness of war and the moral corruption to which it leads is definitely shared by Owen. Owen was deeply uncertain about whether he should have become a conscientious objector. The poem can be seen, then, as a dramatization of Owen's situation: his decision to fight is challenged by arguments which he cannot deny.

The opening sentence of the dead German's speech (15–16) expresses the sentiment which underlies the whole poem. Why does Owen use the word *undone* rather than, say, 'wasted'?

What (26–29) does the German think will now happen in the future?

What (30–38) does he say that he would (and should) have done if he had not decided to fight and thus been killed?

The impact of lines 39–40, which are perhaps the climax of the poem, depends very much on how they are read. Read them aloud and decide what tone of voice best suits their meaning.

W. H. AUDEN

Miss Gee   130

10 *serge:* a strong fabric, usually of worsted
91 *sarcoma:* a malignant tumour, cancer
99 *Oxford Groupers:* members of an evangelical cult

What impression of Miss Gee do you form from reading verses 2–5?

What does the dream (25) suggest about her feelings for the Vicar of St Aloysius? Why does the dream turn into a nightmare? In answering this question think about what the *harsh back-pedal brake* (16 and 35–36) might be taken to symbolize. What explanation does the doctor offer in lines 68–76 for the cause of cancer? Can you see any connection between Miss Gee's feelings for the Vicar and her developing cancer?

What is your reaction to the last four verses? Do you find them funny? Or (consider lines 85–89) rather brutal? Does Auden intend you simply to laugh, or is he suggesting that you should reconsider your own attitude to Miss Gee and people like her?

Miss Gee is written in the form of a ballad. How would you describe the effect of the ballad rhythms and the rhyme scheme? Why does Auden choose to write about Miss Gee's dying in this way?

As I walked out one evening   134

Re-read the first twenty lines. What is the lover saying about the nature of his love? What do you notice about the images used in verses 3, 4 and 5? Do they suggest anything about how realistic the lover is in his beliefs?

Now think about the images used in lines 21–48. What is the implication of lines 27–28? What is the force of the verb *leaks* (30)? What do you think Auden means by *Time will have his fancy* (31) and by the image of the *green valley* covered by *the appalling snow* (33–34)? What, given that we normally associate the word 'bed' with warmth and security, is the significance of the fact that *bed* (42) is made to rhyme with *dead* (44)? How, finally, would you describe Auden's attitude to time in these lines?

The poem ends with three verses which seem to put the earlier part of the poem into a new perspective. Our *distress* should not make us forget that *life remains a blessing* and we should love our *crooked neighbour* with our *crooked heart* (55–56). But what does the adjective *crooked* mean in this context? What does it suggest that we should feel about the nature of human love? How does this picture of human affections compare to the lover's song of the first twenty lines?

What is the significance of the fact that the *deep river* (60) runs on after the lovers have departed?

Dear, though the night is gone   136

What impression of the *room* (3) do you form from the adjective *Cavernous* and the simile *lofty as/A railway terminus* (4–5)?

Is it possible to say what the dream means, or does Auden leave the details deliberately mysterious?

Can this poem be described as a love poem?

Lullaby   136

  6 *ephemeral:* short-lived
15 *Venus:* Goddess of Love

Compare the first verse of this poem to lines 8–20 of *As I walked out one evening*. Where the lover in the previous poem believed that love is eternal, Auden here admits that he is *faithless* (2), and that time will eventually destroy his lover's beauty. The tone of this verse and the whole poem is nevertheless extremely tender (do you agree?). It can, perhaps, be read as an elaboration on lines 55–56 of *As I walked out one evening*.

In verse 2 it is stated that when two people are in love they are made to believe in *supernatural sympathy/Universal love and hope* (16–17). How, though, does verse 3 contradict this vision? Does this mean (read lines 26–30) that the experience of love is meaningless?

What in verse 3 does Auden hope for his lover? Read the verse aloud. How would you describe the tone of these lines?

Musée des Beaux Arts   138

  2 *The Old Masters:* the great painters of the past
  9 *They:* the Old Masters
14 *Breughel:* a famous 16th century Flemish painter
    Icarus: A painting by Breughel of the story of Icarus. In Greek
    mythology Icarus flew too near the sun and fell to his death when
    the wax , which secured his wings, melted. The remaining lines of
    the poem focus on details from Breughel's painting.

What did the Old Masters understand about suffering?

Why (5–8) is the *waiting* of the *aged* (5) put alongside the children *skating/On a pond* (7–8)? Similarly, why is the *dreadful martyrdom* (10) made to *run its course . . . in a corner . . . Where the dogs go on with their doggy life* (10–12)?

How in lines 14–21 do the ploughman, the sun and the ship react to the drama and tragedy of Icarus's death? What does the word *leisurely* (15) add to the poem?

Finally how would you describe the tone of this poem? What does the tone contribute to what Auden is saying about the place of suffering in human life? Do you find any similarities between this poem and any of his love poems?

Epitaph on a Tyrant   138

Written in the 1930s as Hitler's power grew in Germany, this poem suggests that the tyrant is a kind of artist.

What kind of *Perfection* (1) does the tyrant seek? How does the phrase *of a kind* help define Auden's attitude to the tyrant? What do you take the tyrant's *poetry* (2) to be? The last line suddenly introduces a new perspective into the poem. How?

Refugee Blues   139

It is interesting to read this poem about the plight of the Jews in Nazi Germany in the light of a later comment by Auden:

> The novelty and shock of the Nazis was that they made no pretence of believing in liberty and justice for all, and attacked Christianity on the grounds that to love one's neighbour as oneself was a command fit only for effeminate weaklings . . .

The person who is speaking in the poem is a refugee. Note the way in which the third line of each verse has the same structure. Why do you think that Auden repeats the phrase *my dear* throughout the poem? Why within each of these lines does he repeat the initial phrase?

What is the point of the allusions to animals, fish and birds in verses 8, 9 and 10? These allusions culminate in line 30. How should this line be read? Sadly? Ironically? Bitterly? Or how?

The Unknown Citizen   140

  9 *scab:* a worker who refuses to accept official union policy
 26 *Eugenist:* a man who believes that the human race can be improved by carefully selective breeding

Several phrases in the poem: *Greater Community* (5), *Social Psychology workers* (12) are in capital letters. What does this suggest about how Auden intends the reader to respond to the ideas represented by these phrases?

How would you describe this man's life? Why are the questions posed in line 28 *absurd*?

The Shield of Achilles   141

Title: In Greek mythology Thetis, the mother of Achilles, had a shield made for her son Achilles by the lame armourer Hephaestos.

24 *ritual pieties:* ceremonial religious services
26 *Libation:* the pouring of wine in honour of a god
57 *axioms:* self-evident truths

Thetis looks over Hephaestos's shoulder to see what he has carved on the shield. She expects to see a vision of civilized order (2–3), religious ceremony (23–26), or of sport and dance (45–49). What in fact he has carved is a vision of the world as he sees it: a vision which moves backward and forward in time from the Greeks to the present day, but which remains constant in its sense of injustice and cruelty.

Verses 2 and 3 What is the effect of the accumulation of negatives in lines 10–11? Note how line 14: *A million eyes, a million boots in line* deprives the multitude of any kind of individual identity. What do you think Auden means by the adjective *unintelligible* (13)?

The *voice without a face* (16) is similarly impersonal. What does Auden imply by the phrase *Proved by statistics* (17)? What is the reaction of the *multitude* (13) to this voice? What do you think Auden is attacking in these lines?

Verses 5 and 6 What does *Barbed wire* suggest to you in line 31? Comment on the significance of *arbitrary* (31). What is described in lines 34–37?

The phrase *mass and majesty of this world* (38) seems to suggest something important and noble. Do you think, though, reading the rest of the verse, that Auden intends us to understand lines 38–40 in this way? What would be lost if the verb *liked* (42) was replaced by the verb you might have expected: 'wanted'?

Verse 8 The *vacancy* of line 54 is the *weed-choked field* of line 52: an image of disorder. Why does Auden introduce the *ragged urchin* (53) into the poem?

PHILIP LARKIN

Wild Oats   145

The humour of this poem derives very much from Larkin's tone of voice. Consider, for instance, lines 8 and 21, and decide how they should be read aloud.

Also typical of Larkin, and important to the poem, are the circumstantial details of verse 2. What do these details add to the poem?

How would you describe the impact of the last three lines?

Does the poem as a whole strike you as funny or sad or what?

Reasons for Attendance   146

The experience of watching young people at a dance leads the speaker to think about what it is that makes people happy.

First consider his attitude to the dancers. What does his initial reaction (6 and 7) seem to be? What do the phrases *sensing the smoke and sweat* and *The wonderful feel of girls* add to your understanding of his attitude? Does the verb *maul* (18) add a more critical and dismissive note?

In lines 8–10 he seems to reject the idea that sex is the main source of happiness. What is it that he says in lines 12–16 is more important to him? Why is the word *individual* repeated twice in these lines?

How much truth do you think there is in the view that Larkin is poking fun at himself as a middle-aged man who is out of touch with the young people he is watching? You may, of course, decide that Larkin is to some extent laughing at himself and still feel that the poem poses a serious question about what is important and satisfying in life.

What, finally, is the significance of the last line, and, in particular, the last word?

Poetry of Departures   147

   8 *Elemental:* simplifying, reducing to fundamentals
  26 *fo'c'sle:* the crew's quarters on a ship
  27 *Stubbly with goodness:* a reference to the fact that if he dropped out he would be unshaven and therefore leading a natural, 'good', life

Another poem in which the speaker reflects on his own life in the light of other people's actions and decisions.

The second verse makes it clear that the speaker is, to say the least, dissatisfied with his life. What is it that he feels is wrong? (Think, too, about lines 31–32.)

What (verse 3) is the speaker's initial reaction when he hears that someone has *walked out on the whole crowd* (17)? Why does hearing about other people's dramatic actions help him to *stay/Sober and industrious* (23)?

What is it (verse 4) that he objects to in the whole notion of escape?

Church Going   148

13 *lectern:* the desk on which the Bible rests in a church
14 *Hectoring:* bullying, blustering
24 *chronically on show:* on show as a historical record. There is also, perhaps, the suggestion of a 'chronic' disease, a disease which has lasted a long time
25 *pyx:* the box in which the host, or wafer which represents the body of Christ, is kept
30 *simples:* herbs with medicinal qualities
41 *rood-lofts:* the gallery above the rood screen which separated the choir from the nave in some medieval churches
42 *ruin-bibber:* someone who enjoys looking over ruins
44 *myrrh:* a bitter gum which is one of the ingredients of incense
46 *silt:* the fine sediment carried in a river; here used metaphorically to suggest the final remains of the Christian faith
53 *accoutred:* dressed up
   frowsty: musty
56 *blent:* the air is a 'blend' of many different smells

How would you describe the speaker's attitude on entering the church (verses 1 and 2)? What impression of the church is created by the descriptive details?

In verses 3, 4 and 5 the poet speculates on what will happen to churches in the future. What are the possibilities?

What does the speaker mean by describing the church as *A serious house on serious earth* (55)? How does the language and tone of these verses differ from what has gone before?

Although the poem is for the most part conversational in tone, it employs a strict rhyme scheme and metrical form. Can you suggest what this careful and traditional organization adds to the poem? Is the tension between the conversational tone and the formal structure in itself significant?

The Whitsun Weddings   150

28 *pomaded:* with perfumed hair-oil

Travelling by train from Hull to London one Whitsun, Larkin notices the newly-wed couples waiting with their friends and relatives at the stations. The poem begins as a description of the journey and the wedding crowds but gradually develops into a reflection on marriage, the journey becoming an image of the journey through life which these newly-wed couples have elected to make together.

Consider the first two verses and list some of the precise details which
Larkin includes in these verses. Why do you think he begins the poem
in this way? The wedding crowds are described in equal detail. What is
Larkin's attitude to these people? Does he describe them as a neutral
observer? Does he seem to feel superior to them? Or what? In
particular, study the language used in lines 28–30, 36–41 and 48–55.

In the final image (79–80), the excitement and hope of the
honeymooners is compared to a shower of arrows shot somewhere
into the future, *out of sight*. To understand this image you will need to
re-read the poem closely, paying particular attention to lines 19–20,
23–24, 29–33, 54–55, 59 and 66–67. Now write down what you think
the image implies about: a) the marriages of the young couples
b) hope for the future as we travel through life.

Dockery and Son   152

  2 *Dean:* a senior tutor in an Oxford college
 36 *Innate assumptions:* beliefs which are buried deep in us and probably
      inherited from our ancestors
 44 *patronage:* support and protection

Like *The Whitsun Weddings*, this poem begins with the description of a
particular occasion (here the speaker's return to his old Oxford
college). Many of the descriptive details in fact lead very deliberately
towards the bleak conclusion. Consider the following points:
a) The speaker is *Death-suited, visitant* (3). Literally this means that he
     is dressed formally in a black suit for his visit, but there is the
     suggestion that he is a ghost returned from the dead to review his
     former life.
b) The room in which he used to live is locked. It is impossible, that is,
     ever to return to the past: our youth goes from us for ever.
c) There is, perhaps, in the description of the *Joining and parting* (24)
     railway lines a suggestion that our lives are as predetermined as the
     course of the train.

What are the *Innate assumptions* referred to in lines 35 and 36? What
does the image *warp tight-shut, like doors* (38) suggest about *what/We
think truest, or most want to do*? In what sense do our *Innate assumptions
. . . rear/Like sand-clouds* (41–42)?

Finally, how would you describe the speaker's attitude as it emerges in
the poem? Do you personally find the poem unacceptably depressing,
or do you think that Larkin is stating something about life which we
should all face up to?

The Building   153

2 *lucent comb:* the shining crest of the roof
19 *in abeyance:* suspended, no longer important
62 *contravenes:* opposes, counters
64 *propitiatory:* appeasing

Larkin deliberately, of course, avoids telling us that the building is a hospital. The realization comes consequently as something of a shock. Re-read the earlier part of the poem and show how details of the description hint at the true subject without actually naming it.

The initial image of the *lucent comb* suggests that the building might be a church, and there are several further references in the poem to religion. Consider the idea of 'confession' (22), the comparison of the patients to *congregations* (54), and the mention of *cathedrals* (62). Why is it, do you think, that Larkin builds these references into the poem? Are there any similarities between this poem and *Church Going*?

TED HUGHES

The Thought-Fox   157

Hughes has written of this poem that 'every time anyone reads it the fox will get up somewhere out of the darkness and come walking towards them'. (*Poetry in the Making*, p.20.) Re-read lines 9–21 and list the details which help bring the fox alive.

The poem is not, however, simply a description of the fox. Hughes himself comments that it is 'about a fox, obviously enough, but a fox that is both a fox and not a fox'. What does he mean? Consider the implications of the title, think about what is described in the first two verses, and ask yourself what the *It* is which *enters the dark hole of the head* in the last verse.

Wind   158

Hughes's technique is to rely upon a sustained series of images to force the reader to understand and appreciate what it is he is describing. Consider the following images, making sure that you understand how each works and what each contributes to the poem as a whole:
This house has been far out at sea all night (1)
Winds stampeding the fields (3)
At noon I scaled along the house-side as far as/The coal-house door (9)

The tent of the hills drummed and strained its guyrope (12)
The house/Rang like some fine green goblet in the note/That any second would shatter it. (16–18)

What other images add to the poem's descriptive force?

Pike   159

This powerful poem divides into three parts:
Verses 1–4 describe the beauty and fierce destructiveness of the pike. What is the impact of the heavily alliterative and basically monosyllabic opening lines?

What do the word *tigering* and *malevolent* contribute to the first verse, and how, in particular, do they make you feel about the *dance* of line 4?

Explain the image *submarine delicacy and horror* (7).

Verses 5–7 tell the story of what happened to the three pike Hughes apparently kept as a child. What does the anecdote add to your understanding of the pike's nature?

Verses 8–12 move out from another childhood anecdote to a mysterious and terrifying vision of something rising from the *Stilled legendary depth* (33) of the pond. Is Hughes in these lines simply dramatizing his feelings as a child, half-wishing, half-fearing that he had caught a monster pike? Or does the sombre and hypnotic language (consider, for example, the repetitions) suggest that the experience has a more general significance, and, if so, how would you explain this further meaning?

Consider the idea that this poem, like *The Thought-Fox*, is in part a poem about the writing of a poem. According to this reading, the description of the boy fishing is an image of the poet writing. What, in this case, do these last verses tell you about how Ted Hughes views the act of writing a poem?

Full Moon and Little Frieda   160

This beautifully economical description of the *cool small evening* is shot through with a sense of wonder. Little Frieda stands amazed at all she sees while Hughes is equally amazed by his daughter's innocent excitement.

What do the final two lines add to the poem?

Crow Tyrannosaurus   161

2 *cortege:* a funeral procession
16 *blort:* a blast of air
18 *Abbatoir:* slaughter house

Crow Tyrannosaurus is from a volume Hughes published in 1970 called
Crow. There has been a great deal of discussion about both the
meaning and the value of the poems in this collection. In some poems
Crow seems to think and feel as a man, in others he protests against
the horror of man's existence, while in a third group of poems it is he
himself who is responsible for the horror.

In *Crow Tyrannosaurus* Crow is conscious of the disgusting and
terrifying violence of existence, but is inextricably a part of it.

The poem begins with a laconic statement of how life depends on
killing. This statement is developed in verses 2–5. Much of the effect of
these verses stems from the verbs Hughes has chosen. What, for
instance, do the following suggest: *fled* (5), *pulsating* (6), *writhed* (9),
and *gagging* (10)? An incinerator is a furnace used for burning rubbish.
What does this tell you about how man deals with the guilt he feels at
killing?

In verse 6 Crow meditates on whether he ought to withdraw from the
general slaughter. How seriously should we take his deliberations?
Consider the repeated *Alas* (21–22) and the phrase *the light* (24).

Instinct (verse 7) stops his thinking. He hears *Weeping* (28), and, in his
guilt, contributes to it.

What does the way in which the final ten or so lines are set out
contribute to the poem's emotional impact? What do you think
Hughes means to suggest by *the eye's/roundness/the ear's/deafness*?

Re-read *Pike*. Does *Crow Tyrannosaurus* in any way develop the thought
of the earlier poem?

Ravens   162

What is the child's reaction to the dead lamb? Why do you think
Hughes introduces the child into the poem? How would you describe
Hughes's own feelings about the death? How, for instance, does he
write about the dead lamb? – With scientific objectivity? With compassion? Or what? And what do the last seven lines suggest not just about
this death but about life and death generally?

The Stag   164

If you read the poem aloud you will notice that several of the sentences are unusually long. Think in particular about the last two sentences. Why do you think Hughes has written these sentences in this way?

The experience of the stag is placed alongside that of the crowd who have come to watch the hunt. Consider lines 7–11 and the force of the poem's final word: *disappointed*. Is it possible to say anything about Hughes's attitude to the hunt and its spectators?

SEAMUS HEANEY

Digging   167

8 *drills:* ridges of soil with plants (here potatoes) growing in them
18 *Toner's bog:* a peat bog

Heaney has written of this poem:

> *Digging*, in fact, was the name of the first poem I wrote where I thought my feelings had got into words . . . I wrote it in the summer of 1964, almost two years after I had begun 'to dabble in verses'. This was the first place where I felt I had done more than make an arrangement of words: I felt I had let down a shaft into real life . . . I now believe that the *Digging* poem had for me the force of an initiation: the confidence I mentioned arose from a sense that perhaps I could do this poetry thing too, and having experienced the excitement and release of it once, I was doomed to look for it again and again.

What does Heaney mean by the idea of digging with his pen? Do you find the comparison to *a gun* (2) particularly appropriate?

Note how Heaney draws upon several of the senses in establishing the physical detail of this poem, and make a list of which images depend upon which senses.

How would you describe Heaney's attitude to his father and grandfather as expressed in this poem?

Follower   168

5 *wing:* mould-board of a plough
6 *sock:* the detachable part of the plough which cuts into the ground
8 *headrig:* a headland in a ploughed field, i.e. a strip left unploughed at the end of the field

A second poem in which Heaney explores his relationship with his father. Describe Heaney's feelings for his father, as a child and as an adult.

Cow in Calf   169

4 *byre:* cowshed

A descriptive poem remarkable for the cumulative force of its images. Consider each of these images, and explain how each contributes to your sense of what the cow is like.

At a Potato Digging   170

1 *drill:* see note to *Digging* line 8
4 *creel:* basket
25 *humus:* decomposed organic matter in the soil
50 *flotilla:* a fleet of small ships (literally)
57 *Libation:* wine or other liquid poured in honour of a god

The immediate subject here is the digging of potatoes on an Irish farm in the twentieth century, but Heaney's real subject is the relationship which the Irish people have with the land which they depend upon for survival.

Section I What does the verb *swarm* (3) suggest to you? What impression of the labourers is created by the simile comparing them to *crows* (5)? What does the image of fishing (10) add to your understanding of the labourer's work? The phrase *the black/Mother* (11–12) suggests that as they pick the potatoes the labourers seem to be worshipping the earth as they would worship the Virgin Mary. How is this idea developed in lines 11–16?

Section II Heaney describes how the potatoes look, feel and smell. Which of these words and images seem to you particularly effective as description?

Section III This section describes the effects of the great famine of 1845 when the Irish were driven by hunger to eat rotten potatoes. How are the Irish described in lines 30–31? What is the force of the verbs *scoured* and *wolfed* (32 and 33)?

How does the image *beaks of famine* in line 41 emerge from line 38? Is it an effective image?

Why does Heaney compare the Irish to *plants* (43)? What is the meaning of *grafted* (44), and how does it fit into this series of images? What is the force of *Hope rotted like a marrow* (45)?

Section IV The poem ends where it began with a description of potato pickers today. Note, though, the way in which the words *faithless* and *Libations* connect back to the religious imagery of the first verse. Why do you think that Heaney chose to end the poem in this way?

Dedicatory poem from *Wintering Out*   172

2 *camp for the internees:* detention camps set up by the British
   Government for terrorists in the early 1970s
7 *déjà vu:* something you have the sense of having experienced before
8 *Stalag 17:* a German prisoner-of-war camp in the 1939–45 World War

This poem first appeared at the beginning of Heaney's third book of poems, *Wintering Out*. It points to the way in which his later poems focus less on childhood memories than upon what it has been like to live in Northern Ireland since the present troubles began.

How does the last sentence in the poem relate to the joke in line 9?

Punishment   172

 2 *halter:* a rope for leading animals or hanging criminals
 6 *amber:* a yellowish, fossil resin
13 *barked:* peeled or stripped
15 *brain-firkin:* when she was killed the girl was a *sapling*, but the bog
    has turned her bones to *oak*, her head to a *firkin* or small wooden
    cask
34 *combs:* the brain reminds the poet of honeycomb in a hive
39 *cauled:* a caul is a net or covering for the head

In May 1950 two Danish farmers discovered a body in a peat bog. They thought they had found the victim of a recent murder, but in fact the body was 2000 years old, preserved by the peat. Other bodies were found, and Heaney has written several poems about these discoveries.

The girl had been killed for committing adultery, and the depth of Heaney's feeling for her is clear from the poignancy of his description. It is not, however, the simple fact of the girl's death which moves Heaney, for (he has observed the fate of girls in Ireland who have been tarred and feathered for falling in love with British soldiers) the body of this girl raises disturbing questions for him about his role as an artist. He would not have spoken up in *her* defence, and he has failed to protest against the fate suffered by her modern counterparts. As a writer (and an Irishman) he can both *connive/in civilized outrage* (41–42) and *understand the exact/and tribal, intimate revenge* (43–44). The poem explores, then, Heaney's position as a writer in modern Ireland. It exemplifies, moreover, in the moving connection which is made between an Iron Age adultery and a modern political revenge, something of how Heaney has sought to understand the problems of the present in terms of the experience of the past.

Casualty 174

30 *politic:* diplomatic, sensitive
49 *Surplice and soutane:* a surplice is the white linen cloth worn by a clergyman over his 'soutane' or cassock
56 *swaddling band:* the clothes which are wrapped tightly round a small baby. The use of the word here suggests how the funeral removes all adult differences between the participants, binding them tightly in their common origins.
80 *tribe's complicity:* the *tribe* is the Roman Catholic community; *complicity* means being an accomplice. The implication is that every Catholic in Ulster is involved in or at least sympathetic towards the activities of the IRA.
100 *purling:* spinning round
110 *revenant:* ghost

This poem is a meditation on the death of an acquaintance of Heaney's, a Derry fisherman who was killed while breaking the curfew imposed by the Provisional IRA in the aftermath of the Bloody Sunday killings in Londonderry on 30th January 1971 when thirteen Civil Rights demonstrators were shot by the British Army.

The poem is notable for its descriptions of the personality of the murdered fisherman and for its accounts of the two funerals (47–59 and 85–98). Central to the argument are the parallels Heaney draws between the fisherman's refusal to conform to the expectations of the Catholic community and his own isolated position as a poet within that community. The fisherman breaks the curfew (60–64) and the poem revolves round the question which Heaney imagines the other man might put posthumously to him: was he to blame in not conforming to the expectations of the Catholic community – the 'tribe'? By implication it is a question which Heaney himself as a Catholic and a poet writing about the troubles has to face. What balance should he strike, for instance, between understanding and condemnation in writing about the actions of the Provisionals? His answer to these questions is given in lines 100–109, where, in celebrating the fisherman's freedom and the sure rhythms of his craft, he implies that his own *proper haunt* (108) is similarly *Somewhere, well-out, beyond . . .* (109). Compare these last lines to the much more ambiguous note struck in the last verse of *Punishment*.

Now re-read the poem and write down what you can about: the life and personality of the fisherman; Heaney's attitude to him.

GLOSSARY

alliteration	the repetition of a consonant sound at the start of two or more words:
	Pike, three inches long, perfect Pike in all parts. . . .
	Ted Hughes *Pike*
assonance	the repetition of the same vowel sound in a group of words:
	To bend with apples the mossed cottage-trees'
	Keats *To Autumn*
ballad	a poem in story form, normally divided into four line verses rhyming abab
imagery	the technique whereby a writer makes one object stand for another. Thus a red rose is traditionally an image for passionate love.
lyric	a short, personal and usually musical poem
metaphor	a special kind of image in which the characteristics of one object are transferred to another – eg. the phrase 'the ship ploughed the waves', where the ship is imagined to be cutting through the waves as a plough cuts through the soil
simile	another kind of image in which a direct comparison is made between one thing and another:
	Daylong this tomcat lies stretched flat As an old rough mat. . . .
	Like a bundle of old rope and iron Sleeps till blue dusk
	Ted Hughes *Esther's Tomcat*
sonnet	a poem of fourteen ten syllable lines which is usually divided into two sections of eight and six lines respectively
tone	the distinctive quality of a piece of writing which conveys the writer's attitude to his subject-matter or to his readers. The tone of a poem might be, among other things, happy, bitter, nostalgic or ironic.

INDEX OF FIRST LINES

ACKNOWLEDGEMENTS

W. H. Auden: from *Collected Poems*. Reprinted by permission of Faber and Faber Ltd.

T. S. Eliot: from *Collected Poems 1909–1962*. Reprinted by permission of Faber and Faber Ltd.

Seamus Heaney: 'Digging'; 'Follower'; 'Cow in Calf' and 'At a Potato Digging' from *Death of a Naturalist*; 'Dedicatory Poem' from *Wintering Out*; 'Punishment' from *North*; 'Casualty' from *Field Work*. All reprinted by permission of Faber and Faber Ltd.

Ted Hughes: 'The Thought-Fox' and 'Wind' from *The Hawk in the Rain*; 'Pike' from *Lupercal*; 'Full Moon and Little Frieda' from *Wodwo*; 'Crow Tyrannosaurus' from *Crow*; 'Ravens' from *Moortown*; 'The Stag' from *Season Songs*. All reprinted by permission of Faber and Faber Ltd.

Philip Larkin: 'Wild Oats'; 'The Whitsun Weddings' and 'Dockery and Son' from *The Whitsun Weddings*; 'The Building' from *High Windows*. Reprinted by permission of Faber and Faber Ltd. 'Reasons for Attendance'; 'Poetry of Departures' and 'Church Going' are from *The Less Deceived*. Reprinted by permission of The Marvell Press, London.

Wilfred Owen: 'Anthem for Dead Youth' from *The Collected Poems of Wilfred Owen*. Reprinted by permission of Chatto and Windus Ltd. The texts of the poems have been taken from the new edition: *The Complete Poems and Fragments* edited by Jon Stallworthy. (Chatto and Windus/O.U.P. 1983)

W. B. Yeats: from *The Collected Poems of W. B. Yeats*. Reprinted by permission of A. P. Watt Ltd., on behalf of Michael B. Yeats, Anne Yeats and Macmillan, London, Limited.

The author and publishers would like to thank Mr R. B. Kennedy for his advice and assistance during the preparation of the anthology.

The publisher would like to thank the following for permission to reproduce photographs:
BBC Hulton Picture Library, pp.7, 54, 92, 99, 111, 129; Mark Gerson, p.144; Fay Godwin, pp.156, 166; Mansell Collection, pp.40, 65, 82; National Portrait Gallery, pp.32, 121; Trustees of Dove Cottage, p.20.